MURDER IN THE PENTHOUSE

THE PRIVATE INVESTIGATOR ANNIE HUDSON REAL ESTATE MYSTERY SERIES

BOOK 2

VALERIE BRANDY

EMERALD LION
PRESS

🌸 Created with Vellum

CONTENTS

CHAPTER ONE

TONY VASQUEZ DIDN'T LAND with grace when he fell from the balcony of his eleventh floor, ocean-view penthouse apartment.

Hours after he'd taken the plunge, Tony's crumpled form was arranged on the hood of a parked car, where he'd landed with such force the car's front end had caved in on itself. Now, Private Investigator Annie Hudson stood in front of Tony's smashed remains, noting the lack of dignity in his position. One of Tony's arms protruded over the front bumper. A single shoe lay discarded on the pavement. The rest of Tony was buried in the engine well, the fact that he was slightly less visible in such a position his only relief. On this scenic harbor road— marked by soaring seagulls overhead and the light of buildings across the bay— Tony's mangled form was quite a scar.

Annie reviewed what she had already gathered from witness statements about how he had fallen. According to one bicyclist and a pedestrian– both of whom had been touring the harbor at the time– it wasn't a pretty sight. Other victims of falls from similar heights were at least afforded the dignity of a beautiful demise, their arms spread wide like birds in flight, a calm suspension carrying them through their final moments. But not Tony. Tony had flapped his arms in a panic, a tangle of limbs reaching for whatever might stop his descent. His scream was so loud it ricocheted across the night air on this narrow, harbor street in San Diego, and multiple guests at nearby hotels would later claim they heard it with their own ears. He careened through the air like an unwilling bowling ball, his weight dragging him toward the Earth, his fingertips skimming the top of a palm tree as his body landed on a parked sedan with a final, unapologetic thud. The sedan's alarm had blared for twenty minutes afterward, until the owner arrived at a mess of a scene. Police cars. Ambulances. All of them too late to help poor Tony.

"We came here for a favor and you're already putting us to work," FBI Agent Ethan Beckett said, his voice bringing Annie back into the moment. Ethan was standing next to her but also a foot behind, giving her the space he knew she needed. As Annie's only frequent companion, Ethan understood her many quirks— and wanting a comfortable radius of space around her person while she worked was one of them. "Annie said you were a friend, but I'm starting to question if that's the truth." The laughter in his words made it clear no harm was intended.

Beside him, San Diego's Police Chief Melissa Sanchez drank her coffee from a paper cup, unaffected by Tony's crumpled body. To her, this was just another day at the office. "Hey," she shrugged. "San Diego is a busy city for crime. You can't bring the greatest mind into town and not expect us to put it to use."

"I'm surprised no one's settled on suicide as the case's obvious conclusion," Annie said. "No offense meant, of course. It's just—"

"None taken," Chief Sanchez said. "We don't have the bandwidth for the amount of trouble we see. You're right. If it barks like a dog, we're going to call it one. Most falls are jumpers. Plain and simple. I'd bet lunch that's what this is, too. A simple suicide. But his father..."

"Doesn't agree?" Annie asked.

"His father owns the building. He's at the station now. He seems to think this is all tied up in Real Estate. Claims somebody wanted his son's apartment. Suspicious packages had been arriving as well, over the course of many weeks. He thinks it was murder."

"And?" Annie smiled, not one to miss the opportunity to give her friend a needling.

"And," Chief Sanchez ran a hand through her long, waving hair. "Tony's father happens to be a big donor to a certain unnamed elected official's campaign. The same official that appointed me as Police Chief."

"Don't bite the hand that feeds you," Ethan nodded. "Smart choice."

"Look," Chief Sanchez sighed. "Nobody wants to accept their relative was struggling. This, right here?" She motioned at the mess in front of her, eyeing the broken car and the pieces of Tony that were tangled in the engine line. "It's a classic suicide. Open and shut. At the same time, we have to give the impression of due diligence. Meanwhile, I've got other people who need help from us. People who don't have rich Dads. People who are trying to keep their kids outta gangs or getting beat up by their spouses. People with real problems, you see?" She leaned in, her voice lowering. "That's where my heart is. That's who I'm called to help. A case like this is— noise." She waved a hand in the air at nothing in particular. "Still, someone needs to investigate to keep Tony's Dad off my ass."

"And we're the ass-savers," Annie nodded. "Ethan? You up for it?"

"I'm game if you are," Ethan answered. "The FBI has concerns in this area. Lotta trafficking, some DHS action. I can justify the time."

"So, we have a deal?" Chief Sanchez nodded, eager to wrap the meeting up. "I'll tell Tony's Dad we've brought in the world's foremost expert in real-estate-related crime and that you're conducting a thorough investigation."

"You have a deal," Annie agreed. "But I want the scoop on the letter, in return." Annie referenced the reason they'd come to San Diego in the first place. On her last case, Annie had received a letter from an uncatchable serial killer who had been responsible for murdering her brother. The letter was only three words long, but the way Annie had received it told her the killer had access to internal police information. "He was waiting," Annie added. "The person who sent the letter. He was waiting until a case came up that involved my specific niche. Real Estate. He knew before the FBI, which means he's someone on the inside. Or he knows someone on the inside. He watched the cases as they came in—" Annie trailed off, unwilling to say more.

"It'll take some time," Sanchez warned. "Thousands of departments out there. You'll need to let me make some calls."

"We've waited fifteen years," Annie answered. "I'm here for as long as it takes." She paused, thinking of her friend's safety. "You'll want to be discreet. He could be one of your own. It would explain how he's evaded being identified."

"Don't you worry about me," Chief Sanchez smiled. "I can handle myself. We have a deal." Chief Sanchez extended a hand and Annie shook it, the two women striking a deal based on mutual respect and necessity.

"Now," Annie leaned down, staring at Tony like he was a friend, her eyes pained. "Let's find out who killed Tony."

"You don't think it was a suicide?" Chief Sanchez balked, a little annoyed at Annie's resistance to entertain the most obvious of answers.

"No," Annie shook her head. "His father is correct. He was murdered." She looked up at the tall building in front of her, from which Tony had fallen. It was an eleven-story, upscale apartment building, perched on the edge of the water. San Diego was one of the world's most expensive cities, and real estate like the building in front of Annie was half the reason. Double doors marked the entryway, modern pillars holding up an awning with the building's name written in pretentious script: *Rowling Heights.* From its lofty upper floors, the best units in Rowling Heights overlooked the San Diego harbor, their occupants privy to a secret cycle of orange sunsets and yellow dawns. Across the harbor, moored sailboats bobbed up and down, their sails tucked safely away in case the wind picked up. An occasional seagull made its way toward the edge of the harbor's defensive cliffs. To the East, a collection of similar buildings reached for the sky, the lights of their windows steady and sure. Their noticeable opulence and the gentle hush of waves drove home the point: living at Rowling Heights meant more than an apartment. This place wasn't just a location. It was an *experience.* One worth paying for. And Tony? He had paid with his life.

"I'll need to speak to the residents," Annie said. And with that, her investigation began.

CHAPTER TWO

CATALINE

ON THE SEVENTH floor of *Rowling Heights*, Cataline had been helping her son with his homework when Tony Vasquez's body went careening past their living room window. It had happened so fast that neither Cataline nor her son— Mario— had immediately understood the seriousness of the moment. They were crouched over the living room coffee table, twelve problems into Mario's math homework, when they both heard a strange cry from outside. By the time they looked up, a blur of a thing passed by in a zoom. Cataline's first thought had been that the falling creature was a large, disoriented bird. It wasn't until she heard the car alarm down below that she considered the bird might have been a person. The sound made her peek out the window— seven stories down— where she saw a smashed sedan and a broken body lying on top of it. For the next several hours, Cataline had struggled to keep Mario away from the traumatizing scene down below, neither of them daring to look at the smashed figure so many stories beneath them.

"But I'm old enough," Mario insisted, trying to push the curtains aside so he could see what had happened. Mario had recently turned thirteen and thought the age held much greater significance than twelve.

"*Mijo*," Cataline answered, "No one is ever old enough to see such a thing." She didn't know how to explain to him that one day he would wish there were someone to shield him from the pain of the world. There was no way to tell a child what all adults knew— that growing up simply meant wishing to be young again. Cataline had seen the worst of the world, and her greatest hope was to protect Mario from the same. Every time her son left the house, Cataline said a prayer for him to avoid trouble, but also that any trouble he did encounter was working toward his benefit in some way. Because, although she had seen the worst of the world, Cataline had also seen its best. She found it every day in the eyes of her son, and she knew God could bring beauty out of struggle. She absent-mindedly reached for a crucifix that dangled from a chain around her neck, reminding herself of the power of faith in difficult times.

"What will happen now?" Mario asked.

"I don't know," Cataline said, thinking about the disorder in the world and what it all meant. "We can't see the bigger picture. We can only trust things will work themselves out. *El amor todo la puede*," she said, repeating the phrase she always used when the world didn't make sense. "Love conquers all." Cataline sighed, shaking away the goosebumps that prickled on her arms. "Go play a video game," Cataline said to Mario. "Enough homework for now."

Mario did as he was told, and Cataline pulled out her cell phone, ready to go to work. As the building's manager, Cataline knew everyone. The owner of *Rowling Heights*, Ferdinand Vasquez, had hired her twelve years ago to live on the premises and attend to every issue that arose, and Cataline had done so faithfully, grateful that the deal included free housing. She'd been given the most undesirable unit in the building as part of her compensation. It was a small, cramped apartment with a view of the harbor that was heavily obscured by a nearby housing development. But the apartment provided two bedrooms and was located in San Diego's finest public school district, which meant Mario was getting the kind of education that cost other parents thousands of dollars in private school fees. In return for the apartment and a salary, Cataline offered tours of vacant units, scheduled service requests, engaged in routine property maintenance, ensured the cleaning and security teams were doing their jobs, and generally kept *Rowling Heights* running. As far as jobs that didn't require a degree went, it was the best position in San Diego, and Cataline had gone out of her way to excel.

Immediately, Cataline called 911. She reported the incident with as much detachment as possible. She couldn't be sure whether the person who fell had fallen from *Rowling Heights*, or one of the other nearby buildings in the area. She didn't want to implicate the building in an unnecessary scandal, and— as the 911 operator breezily informed her— multiple calls had come in from up and down the block.

Next, Cataline called her boss, Ferdinand Vasquez, the building's owner. She waited, but his phone rang twice and then went to voicemail. She tried him again but received no response. She sent him a text:

"Someone fell from up high. Not sure if it was our building or the Mayfair. Police called."

Outside, the sound of sirens blared, their red and blue lights reflecting off the boats in the harbor. Cataline stood at the window, watching as the officers attended to the scene, a white cloth laid over the figure. She again took to her phone, opening her email inbox and sending a notice to residents:

"Notice: Police activity outside the building on Wayfair Avenue. Please be aware if you are coming or going, you may need to enter the garage from the other side of the street. We will update all residents as we receive more information."

Cataline felt a weight lift once the email had been sent. She wondered if she should go downstairs and speak to the officers, but worried she'd be implicating *Rowling Heights* in a situation that might not involve the building at all. That was one downside of having a job she loved— Cataline always worried about losing it.

Especially now, she thought to herself, her mind flashing to a new development that had put her on edge recently. Just six months ago, a new tenant had moved into the building. This new tenant's presence had made Cataline consider, for the first time, leaving everything she'd built here. But instead, she had stayed. Because staying was what was good for Mario.

For the rest of the evening, Cataline kept Mario focused on other things as best she could. She let him choose what show they would put on television. She ordered them both a pizza for dinner. Outside, the sounds of police sirens blared, their red and blue lights reflecting off the boats in the harbor. Cataline told herself the jumper was probably someone who had leapt off one of the cheaper buildings on the block, or— even if they had jumped from *Rowling Heights*— perhaps the person was a guest of a tenant. Not anyone she knew. No one who lived in a building as spectacular as *Rowling Heights*— where their every need was met—could ever find themselves unhappy enough to do such a thing.

Finally, Cataline's phone rang, her boss's name lighting up the screen. She answered at once.

"Ferdinand," she started to say. "*Es horrible*! Something terrible has happened..."

Cataline stopped speaking when she heard a choking noise on the other end. Her boss, a gruff, difficult man with a stiff exterior, was crying.

"*Mi mijo*. The man who they say jumped. It was Tony. It was my son."

Cataline gasped. Ferdinand's son, Tony, lived in the penthouse apartment at the top of the building. He was a shy man, not older than thirty. He wasn't good with people, but he'd had everything to live for. His father's wealth afforded Tony access to the best the world had to offer. Cataline couldn't believe Tony would have done such a thing.

But then, the puzzle pieces fell into place. Like machine gears clicking into formation, Cataline realized that Tony might not have jumped. And something she'd seen earlier in the day—something she couldn't possibly ever share—might have been connected to Tony's death.

"Cataline," Ferdinand asked, his voice wavering. "They want me to ask if you saw anything? Anything at all?"

Cataline didn't answer. She let the words flap in the breeze, like the sails on the boats that floated across the harbor. She wished she could ride one of those boats into the sunset, leaving everything behind except for Mario, starting again somewhere new.

Mario. His name echoed in her ears. Cataline glanced at her son, who had finished the last slice of pizza and was once again attending to his math homework, without any prompting from Cataline. He was a good kid. The kind of kid parents prayed for. He did well in school. He was kind to others. And he trusted Cataline more than she trusted herself.

Cataline realized there was no way to tell Ferdinand what she'd seen without the answer harming Mario. She should wait until she was certain, she told herself, promising she could always change her mind at a later date. She debated for a moment, then did what she knew was necessary to protect the only person who mattered to her in this world.

"Nothing. I didn't see anything," Cataline said. "Ferdinand... I'm so sorry."

She wished Ferdinand could know how much she meant it.

CHAPTER THREE

MINDY

WHEN TONY VASQUEZ'S body slammed into the sedan, Mindy Wellington was safely tucked away in her apartment on the ninth floor of *Rowling Heights*, thinking of ways to ruin her ex-husband's life. She'd been sitting in front of paperwork from her lawyer when she'd heard the scream from overhead, her pen scratching notes about taking a more aggressive strategy. Mindy was currently in the process of a nasty divorce and spent most of her evenings on the phone with her lawyers or marking up documents they'd provided. It was the kind of divorce marked not by maturity and grace, but by an utter hatred for the other person that surpassed all logical arguments in favor of a truce. Mindy's husband— Hathaway Wellington— came from a legacy of old money. She'd married him when she was very young because she believed he could show her the best of the world and, in exchange, Mindy was willing to take care of the kids and the home while waiting for love to grow between her and Hathaway. But the kids never came, and— against Mindy's youthful expectation— neither did the love. Instead, thirty years zipped by, and Mindy found herself fifty years old and in an unfulfilling marriage. She was repulsed by the man she had married, a reaction caused by the way he treated her as a replacement mother. Mindy had spent years finding his missing socks. She'd endured countless hours listening to Hathaway whine about his inability to be promoted to partner at the tenth law firm he worked at, biting her tongue so as not to remind him he was only hired because of his father's connections. In Hathaway, Mindy found herself permanently attached to a weak man who had never been tested by the world. He'd never had to make something of himself.

For someone who had come from money, Hathaway lacked any ability to multiply it or hold onto it. It was Mindy who had taken the savings account gifted to them on their wedding day and turned it into ten times more through day trading. It was Mindy who had made sure Hathaway didn't lose his job for failing to show up to the office because he was in one of his many moods. It was *Mindy* who had made sure Hathaway's briefcase was packed each morning, and who reminded him to review his documents before a meeting. Mindy had spent so much time building up and supporting Hathaway that one morning she woke up, and realized she missed someone:

Herself.

She missed who she used to be before she'd given so much time to a partnership that wasn't much about being partners at all.

And so, Mindy had packed a few bags in the middle of the night while Hathaway was dead asleep, unaware his life was about to change forever. Hathaway and Mindy had been renting an expensive apartment on the tenth floor of *Rowling Heights.* They'd moved into the place when Hathaway had temporarily lost yet another job at a middle-class law firm, causing them to liquidate the house they owned and move from home ownership to renting. The rent was more than they should have paid, but they were used to a certain lifestyle, and *Rowling Heights* provided a similar accommodation. Mindy thought about that fact on the night she left him, wandering through the apartment, grabbing her clothes and a few pieces of memorabilia from the hall closet. She stuffed it all in a Balenciaga tote bag, wondering if leaving Hathaway would mean losing whatever quality of life she'd built so far by puppeteering her pathetic husband across San Diego's society scene.

And then, it had hit Mindy: maybe she didn't have to change her lifestyle at all.

She marched out the door to their apartment, letting it shut with a soft click behind her. Tote bag in hand, Mindy stepped into the elevator, checking her reflection in the marbled glass walls that kept her contained, an animal in a cage. She was a woman on a mission, and no man would set her back.

There was a dinging sound as she reached the lobby level, and her slippers padded across the smooth granite floors. She stopped at the door to the security office, banging on its exterior. The door swung open, revealing the building's head of security, Alfred.

"Miss Wellington," Alfred said, trying to pretend he hadn't seen her on the hallway cameras and didn't know she was coming. "What can I do for you—"

"The vacant apartment on the ninth floor," Mindy answered, cutting right to the chase. "I want to rent it."

"That would be a question for Miss Cataline," Alfred said, thinking of the building's manager and the little respect she was afforded by its many residents. "She can set up a tour, perhaps in the morning..."

"I'd like to stay there tonight," Mindy said. "I'll pay immediately. But I can't spend—" her voice started to break. "I simply can't spend— another moment— in that apartment with *him.*"

There was a pause as Alfred took it all in and tried to

make sense of it. "I'll see what I can do," he nodded, picking up the phone to call Cataline. He knew she had a son and hated to interrupt her in the middle of the night, but at *Rowling Heights* the residents generally received whatever they asked for, as long as they could provide the funds to back up the request.

Behind her tears, Mindy breathed a sigh of relief. The team at *Rowling Heights* was nothing if not accommodating. Alfred and Cataline would take care of her, and she wouldn't even have to leave her home. Not really.

Everything was going to be okay.

And it was okay, for quite some time. Months passed by, and Mindy lived on the ninth of *Rowling Heights* while her soon-to-be-ex-husband lived on the tenth floor. Their divorce was in progress and acrimonious. Hathaway's family had hired every lawyer possible to make sure Mindy didn't see a dime. But Hathaway's hatred had only made Mindy surer of her decision. She had done the right thing. At least, she thought so. Until the evening when she heard Tony Vasquez's scream, followed by the car alarm outside, and ran to the window to see what had happened.

There, she saw Tony Vasquez's body crumpled on the outline of a sedan. Her breath quickened. At first, Mindy wasn't sure it was Tony. Blood obscured his features, and the angle of his body made it impossible to confirm his form. But then, Mindy noticed the jacket he was wearing. It was red leather and one she recognized well.

Mindy's heart sunk. She gripped the windowsill, her knuckles turning white. A lump formed in her throat, but Mindy refused to cry out. Tears streamed down her cheeks, and she let her knees fold, her body sliding down against the window into a seated position on the floor.

"Tony," she whispered, her fingertips numb. "What on Earth have you done?"

She thought about the secrets she shared with Tony. She

wondered if they'd led to his demise. If they had, there was nothing she could say. Mindy wanted to see his death avenged, but to win such a battle would inevitably mean losing the war.

Mindy leaned her head against the wall, noting the sound of sirens in the distance. The police would arrive shortly. Perhaps they would want to interview residents of the building.

Mindy's heart sank, and she knew without a doubt— she could never tell them the truth. Because the truth would ruin everything. She reached a hand to her neck and left it there, thinking about what needed to be done.

CHAPTER FOUR

HATHAWAY

ON THE TENTH floor of *Rowling Heights*, Hathaway was sitting on the couch smoking a cigar and watching exotic fish blob up and down in his aquarium when Tony Vasquez's scream interrupted the quiet moment he'd afforded himself. Since Mindy had moved out of the apartment they shared on the tenth floor of *Rowling Heights*, Hathaway had decided to make the place his own. This mainly meant breaking any rule she had created. Mindy didn't like him to smoke cigars inside the home? Now, Hathaway enjoyed a crisp Cuban cigar every other evening. Mindy never wanted him to bring home a pet? Hathaway went to the nearest fish store and procured a large aquarium, filling it with expensive and rare tropical fish. Anybody else might have adopted a dog, but one positive quality Hathaway possessed was an awareness of his limitations. Hathaway knew he was not equipped to care for a creature as time-consuming as a dog. Even a cat would've asked to much of him. That was one of the best things about Hathaway— he never pretended to be anything he wasn't.

If anyone had asked him, Hathaway would have told them honestly that he'd grown up with so many of his needs taken care of as a child, that he didn't exactly know how to take care of himself, let alone anyone else. As their acrimonious divorce progressed, Mindy had made it clear in court documents and statements that she felt deceived by Hathaway. When she married him, she'd thought she was marrying an independent, fully-functioning adult. But if she had asked him, Hathaway would have *told* her didn't know the first thing about how to take care of oneself without a wait-staff, or a team to keep things moving. He thought she had noticed this while dating him and had told himself she loved him anyway. Instead of seeing Hathaway for who he really was, Mindy had painted a picture of the man she wanted over his face. And now... that was supposed to be his problem.

Hathaway reached for a carton of fish food and popped open the lid, only to find that it was empty inside, devoid of the nutritional beads that promised his tropical pets a better life. He tossed the carton in the trash and grabbed his cell phone out of his pocket, hitting a number that was on speed dial. The name, *"Cataline,"* appeared on the screen.

"Cataline— could you call for some of that fish food?" Hathaway said as soon as he heard the building manager's voice on the other line. "Yes, I know it's after hours. Just the same as last time. Tomorrow would be perfect, just leave it by my door." There were some niceties exchanged, and then Hathaway hung up. He knew his request was outside the typical bounds of the services a building manager provided, but he paid such exorbitant fees at *Rowling Heights* that he didn't feel guilty making the smallest of requests. Besides, he thought, Cataline always seemed willing to help him, and had become a kind of replacement for his wife since the separation. And goodness knows, Hathaway needed the help.

At fifty-five years old, Hathaway was being forced into a big, new adventure. He had never lived alone and had moved straight from his family's mansion into an upscale ranch-style home with Mindy. His family had purchased the home for them, just as they had helped Hathaway get through law school with an expensive suite of personal tutors. Hathaway's father had helped him find a route into multiple firms around the area, and— when Hathaway flunked out of one firm— he was swiftly moved into another. But now that Hathaway had failed in a marriage, no one could help him. He realized rather quickly that it was time he helped himself.

And so, Hathaway was determined to "win" his divorce. There was a prenuptial agreement in place, of course, but Mindy had decided to challenge it, and Hathaway was determined to make sure she received nothing as a result. Hathaway didn't want his soon-to-be ex-wife to touch a single, red cent. Not after the way she'd pretended to love him, only to abandon him further down the road.

Hathaway watched the fish spin around his aquarium, counting the red and blue stripes on one particularly exotic species. On another, he noted the white spots that dotted the creature's enormous dorsal fin. He considered that his many fish would never leave him, and he wished for a moment his life were as simple as theirs. But Hathaway knew he wasn't destined for such simplicity. Due to his divorce, he couldn't live at peace like a fish. Because of the divorce, Hathaway had to become a shark.

And earlier tonight, Hathaway had done something so predatory and illegal, that he had even surprised himself. He secretly delighted in the rush of individual subterfuge. Hathaway smiled to himself. For someone who had never taken care of his own needs before, Hathaway was certainly catching on quick.

Just then, he heard an echoing scream and the sound of a car alarm outside. He moved to the window, staring straight down instead of out at the ocean, as he usually did this late at night. Below him— ten floors down— was the crumpled form of a human body, smashed against the hood of a sedan.

Tony Vasquez, Hathaway thought to himself. He recognized the red leather jack donning Tony's form only because he had seen it himself earlier that very evening. He had noticed the jacket hanging over the edge of a chair in Tony's living room, where he had been mere hours earlier.

And now, barely half a day after Hathaway had been inside Tony's apartment without his permission— Tony was dead.

It occurred to Hathaway that he had accidentally stepped into a mess. And for once, he might have to clean it up himself.

CHAPTER FIVE

ALEJANDRO

ALEJANDRO WAS ORGANIZING his closet when Tony's scream emanated from outside his living room window. Located on the eighth floor of *Rowling Heights*, Alejandro's apartment was one of the finest in the building, second only to the penthouse, which was unavailable and occupied by Tony on the day Alejandro signed his lease. If the penthouse had been vacant Alejandro would have scooped it up, but he settled for second best to live in the fanciest building in town. Alejandro appreciated the finer things in life, and he'd chosen to live in *Rowling Heights* because it was the most expensive building he could find near San Diego's harbor. The apartment reflected Alejandro's preference for the high life. A gold-framed mirror hung above an in-wall fireplace. Marble floors stretched from room to room. White furniture filled the space, making it clear in its impracticality that this was a home subject to the assistance of a cleaning service. In the kitchen, a glass shelving system held bottles of tequila, all of them emblazoned with the label *La Vida Liquors*, the name of Alejandro's custom tequila brand. Alejandro told everyone about his liquor business, from strangers in the grocery store to any new potential investor he met at a party. It was the source of his wealth, he'd tell them. As far as Alejandro was concerned, the stuff was liquid gold.

If Alejandro's first love was Tequila, his second was clothing. He considered himself a collector of high-fashion items hand-crafted in Italy or France. On his travels abroad and when shopping in town, Alejandro purchased items made from the finest of fabrics. Nothing he wore was off-label or made in China. Alejandro had connections to the wealthiest communities in San Diego, and he always made sure to look like he belonged in any room he entered. When it came to personal style and grooming, Alejandro was meticulous. That's why— when Tony fell from overhead— Alejandro was seated on the floor of his enormous walk-in closet, tossing items into piles. One corner was reserved for pants. Another corner was the sorting section for dress shirts. And still another was earmarked for suits and blazers. Alejandro pulled a rather gaudy button-down off its hanger, holding it up in front of himself and taking a glance in the mirror. It featured a uniquely horrifying print, emblazoned with sequins spiraling in a paisley pattern.

"Maybe," Alejandro muttered to himself, tossing the shirt into a pile. In the background, a Latin pop song played, creating a kind of wistful nostalgia as Alejandro remembered his younger years on the club scene. Now in his forties, Alejandro liked to credit his younger, more ambitious self for conducting the necessary networking to bring him to his current level of accomplishment. He had built his business through connections made in crowded rooms where bodies churned to pulsing music under the steady flash of lights. Men. Women. Alejandro found them all attractive, especially when they could help him with his entrepreneurial pursuits. He had arrived in this country with nothing, and now— he was a liquor label owner, living a lifestyle others could only dream of. And it would never have happened if he hadn't made sure to meet the right people. Alejandro was nothing if not a man who understood it wasn't *what* a person knew, but *who* a person knew that determined how far they got in life.

When the car alarm sounded from down below, Alejandro was snapped out of his musings. He didn't immediately connect the scream he'd heard with the alarm, although one had followed the other with such immediacy they almost overlapped. He abandoned the closet project, walking shirtless into the living room and standing in front of the floor-to-ceiling windows that looked out over the harbor. He glanced down, just making out the shape of a mottled car and a broken body lying on top of it.

The body was wearing a red leather jacket. Alejandro gulped, realizing that the body had to belong to Tony, and all of this was very, *very* bad news.

He glanced at the Tequila bottles lined up in his kitchen, each one glimmering and pristine, a warrior ready for battle.

Just another connection, Alejandro assured himself, thinking about what he would say if the police came knocking. Alejandro had been telling stories his entire life, winning people over to get him to where he was today. He told himself that this instance wasn't any different, but couldn't help another glance at Tony's crumpled form, thinking about that red leather jacket, and what it meant for him.

CHAPTER SIX

MONTANA

WHEN THE POLICE arrived to clean up the scene where Tony's body had fallen, Montana was across the street at a pizza place, ordering a slice. Montana was a gruff man in his mid-forties with a handlebar mustache, a license to carry, and pock-marked cheeks that didn't dull his unique allure.

Montana shifted in the metal restaurant chair, feeling lucky that dining al fresco on the pizza place's patio gave him a perfect view of the dramatic scene unfolding before him. Montana had lived at *Rowling Heights* for less than a year, and had made it an immediate priority upon move-in to figure out which nearby restaurants were to be counted on for a good time. It seemed that tonight, however, he had guessed wrong. He watched as red and blue lights coated the little harbor road he called home, noting the number of squad cars — six, exactly— and the coroner's van. Montana took another bite of his pizza and a swig of his beer, so unaffected by the scene it looked as if he were watching a football game. As a Department of Homeland Security or "DSH" agent, Montana had witnessed his fair share of travesties. He worked at the border every day, finding new horrors on a regular basis. Last week, the nightmare of choice was a group of human traffickers leaving their victims in a secret compartment beneath a truck bed, a few of them dying from heat and lack of air. The week prior, it was the cartel sending a human mule into the station with a gram of cocaine in his stomach. When the bag exploded, the man's life was lost, and there was nothing anybody could do but pray over him. Montana had seen the worst of humanity and, over time, had hardened himself so as to remain unaffected by it. The tattoos that decorated his arms had grown with his indifference, and now, whenever he went to get a piece of new ink, Montana barely noticed the needle. It was the same way with tragedy. Just another mark.

Montana waved a hand at the waiter. "Another," he said, pointing at the empty glass in front of him. The waiter trotted off to refill his beer, and Montana considered how life was set up. The world, in his eyes, was a game of power. Those who had power lived excellent lives. They got to live in buildings like *Rowling Heights*, and continue to watch the years pass with ease. Those who didn't have power languished away, always struggling for the next small win only to see it wiped out by a loss, or a market failure. When Montana started his job at the DHS, he believed in "us" and "them." It was the government— the good guys— against people who he viewed as a threat to national security. But now, Montana's views had changed. After years of service, he saw little difference between his own country's leadership, the immigrants trying to enter the states, and the cartels across the border. All of it— in Montana's eyes— was just about power.

Montana watched as the coroner lifted the body off the hood of the car, its limbs hanging loose, an unrecognizable face covered in blood. Montana recognized the red leather jacket the body was wearing. Between that and the man's build, it was clear the man who'd jumped was Tony. who lived in the penthouse. Montana had crossed paths with him multiple times and knew him as the owner's son.

As the heir to a real estate empire, Tony had power. Great

power. That was the true travesty, here. Unlike Montana, Tony had been born with power. He wasn't like Montana, who had worked for every square inch of muscle he'd gained in life. Tony had gained everything up front, but he hadn't known how to hold on to it. Montana would have almost felt sorry the guy that he'd lost the race, if only he hadn't had such a head start to begin with.

Montana sighed, removing his cell phone from his jacket pocket. He pressed an icon for speed dial, waiting through the first ring until he heard a familiar click on the other end that told him his contact had been waiting.

"We may have a problem," Montana said. Across the street, the coroner loaded Tony's body into the transport van, the double doors closing with a firm, final thud.

CHAPTER SEVEN

ALFRED

ON THE GROUND FLOOR LOBBY, Alfred was sitting in his office when he heard the news about Tony's fall. As the maintenance and security director of *Rowling Heights*, Alfred answered to the manager, Cataline, and made sure that the building was kept clean and secure. The building's owner, Ferdinand, liked to ensure operating costs were kept at a minimum by hiring staff that were willing to perform more than one job. Ferdinand's penny-pinching meant that Alfred was responsible for overseeing a cleaning crew of three maids, as well as a small security team of rotating private guards, and all the technological security elements such as cameras and keycards.

The broad job description was reflected in the chaotic decor style in Alfred's office. Broken security cameras lay discarded in a pile, their frayed cords sticking out as if begging to be repaired. A bucket, mop, and broom leaned against the far wall, positioned next to a "cleaning in progress" foldable sign. A metal desk was pushed against the western wall, a matrix of monitors displaying different areas of the building laid out across its surface. Behind the desk, Alfred arranged his plump body on an office chair, writing something down on a notepad in front of him. A man in his late sixties, Alfred had been with the building for more than twenty years, providing loyal service to its residents. Alfred didn't have his own children and felt spiritually connected to *Rowling Heights* and the people within. Alfred was more than the head of security. Throughout the years, he had wiped residents' tears, offered counsel in their darkest moments, and kept their secrets when it mattered most. Alfred was a man who could be counted on, and he did the job because it gave him a sense of purpose. Assisting the wealthy was in his blood, if his family legacy was to be believed. His own father had immigrated to San Diego from the United Kingdom, and had claimed when Alfred was a child that their ancestors had been courtiers to more than one British monarch.

On his best days, Alfred considered taking everything he had learned in his years of service and writing a book about what it meant to look after others. In the interest of the task, he kept long, hand-written notes to pass the time. Tonight, he was working on one such document, allowing his pen to scribble manually across a tattered old notebook, recording a recent encounter with one of the residents and what it had meant to him. He was three pages in and lost in thought when his phone buzzed. He paused, putting down his pen to look at the screen.

There, a message waited for him, sent from Cataline. *"Don't look at the street feed before I call you."*

Alfred blinked, considering. He rarely did as he was told, and considered himself above the rule of law when the building he so dearly loved was at risk. He wheeled his chair forward and typed into the keyboard in front of him. The monitor on his far left switched perspectives, revealing a view of *Rowling Heights* from the exterior sidewalk. There, a collection of squad cars circled a four-door sedan parked on the curb. The street was roped off with yellow emergency tape, and coroners wheeled a gurney toward a van, a black tarp covering the form that lay on its surface.

The sound of another notification chimed from Alfred's cell phone. He glanced down at the message from Cataline.

"Seriously, Alfred. Wait for my call. Five minutes."

Alfred shook his head. Cataline knew him well and their working relationship was not just one of partners, but of friends. They shared a mutual love for the building.

He picked up his phone and typed a response. *"Who?"*

The message was simple. Alfred prayed it wasn't a resident. Each one of them was a person he was responsible for, and he hated to think he had failed them in some way.

Three dots appeared in the text message box before Cataline's answer arrived.

"Tony."

Alfred gasped. Tony was the building owner's only son. As someone who had been in Ferdinand's employ for decades, Alfred knew what Tony had meant to him. He would be shattered.

Another message appeared from Cataline:

"On with Ferdinand. He thinks it's murder. Believes it's related to the package issue. Police coming tomorrow. Let's meet early. 6 a.m.?"

The package issue, Alfred thought to himself. He was aware of what Cataline was referencing. For many months, the building had been receiving strange packages, unmarked with any recipient name or apartment number. The boxes arrived in the mail room, stacked and ready to be distributed, before they were swiftly removed and disappeared without a trace. Alfred had placed a security camera in the mail room to try and apprehend the culprit but had only managed to secure video footage of someone in a black hoodie, unloading boxes from the mailroom in the middle of the night into a crate with wheels. Alfred's cameras had dutifully recorded the nightcrawler's path through the elevator and to the roof, where the anonymous individual unloaded the crate and left the packages, as if to store them there, exposed to the elements and wholly visible beneath the night stars. Upon reviewing the footage, Alfred had of course headed straight to the building's rooftop to apprehend the suspect but had found only the sad remains of cardboard boxes, flattened and left out to whither, their contents emptied hours earlier. Since then, Alfred had begun locking the mailroom door at night, and had also locked the door that led to the rooftop, barring all residents from any access to the space whatsoever. His efforts had seemed to alleviate the problem. At least, for now.

Suddenly, Alfred remembered something. The thought flashed before his eyes and refused to leave, overstaying its welcome like an unpleasant dinner guest. Alfred leaned into his security camera system and typed something into the keyboard, reversing the footage to a timestamp earlier that evening, just a few hours before Tony had taken his deathly plunge.

Alfred rewatched the footage, colors from the screen casting blue and gold shadows on his face. A recording of the hallway outside Tony's apartment appeared, the ornate carpeting and wallpapered corridor as familiar to Alfred as that of his own home. Alfred allowed the video to play, and as he watched what unfolded, he brought a hand to his mouth, horror etched across his gentle features. He paused, then rewound, watching the footage one more time as if hoping it might change.

It was exactly as he had seen only hours earlier. When he had witnessed the event then, he had thought it nothing more than a mild curiosity— something he would follow up on at a later date. But now that he understood Tony Vasquez had died only hours later, what Alfred had seen took on a horrible new meaning.

Alfred considered what the footage's release might mean for the residents of the building, who he loved as dearly as if they were his own. It would hurt them and destroy the very soul of *Rowling Heights*. Alfred tried to convince himself the police wouldn't ask to see the video, but he knew any detective worth their salt would demand to review the security footage as a first act of business.

Alfred considered. He knew what he had to do. He let one finger hover over the left arrow button on his keyboard and allowed the other to float over the delete key. He took a deep breath before pushing both buttons at the same time, watching as the recorded tape moved backward, the screen becoming nothing but a vision of static black and white lines.

When it was done, Alfred played the tape forward, ensuring he hadn't missed anything. And just like that— in a momentary decision by the man who kept *Rowling Heights* safe— the video of the corridor outside Tony's apartment was deleted, erasing all record of what happened in the hallway that led to his doorstep only moments before his death.

Alfred felt a stab of regret surge through his chest, but he pushed it down at once. He knew he had done the right thing. His job was to keep the residents of *Rowling Heights* safe, and he would go to whatever lengths necessary to meet the demands of such a high calling.

He picked up his phone and wrote a brief message to Cataline:

"Tomorrow at 6 a.m. it is."

His stomach churned as he thought of his employer, and he knew nothing at *Rowling Heights* would ever be the same again.

CHAPTER EIGHT

POLICE CHIEF SANCHEZ placed an enormous coffee mug in front of Detective Annie Hudson, who peered over its edge with a dissatisfied grimace. "Foam?" Annie asked, aghast. "What happened to the days of no-frills?"

"It's the cappuccino maker," Chief Sanchez answered. "We've spared no expense."

"I'll say," FBI Agent Ethan Becket agreed. "You guys make the FBI headquarters look like a prison cell." He motioned through a set of glass windows into the main processing room of the San Diego Police Department's central hub. Ornate tiles patterned a trail up the walls. Overhead, a painted ceiling insert provided a visual story of the founding of San Diego, told entirely in pictures. The mural depicted San Diego's agrarian past, following its evolution to the urban present, and looked to be painstakingly created by hand. Officers milled about their desks, a relaxed, collegial atmosphere dominating the room.

"It's a tough city, but no one can say it's not well-funded," Police Chief Sanchez took a seat at a long wooden table in the room they'd commandeered. "San Diego is one of the most expensive cities in the US," she added. "Trust me. Keeping this place safe? We've earned a few perks."

"I'll say," Annie agreed. She sipped the coffee, trying to look pleased with the result. Ethan stifled a smile. He knew Annie preferred the basics in life and found any additional fluff— including decorative coffee foam— to be an insulting rejection of utility. "Should we get down to it?" She added in her short, odd little way.

"Absolutely," Chief Sanchez agreed. She slid a stack of files across the desk, laying them out as she addressed the contents of each. "This is the basics of the case— what we know so far. This right here is some background on the building, provided by the victim's father. He's more than willing to cooperate, so you won't face any roadblocks there. The final file is everything we were able to pick up on Tony Vasquez. The guy is clean as a whistle. Not so much as a traffic ticket," she paused as if considering whether she should elaborate. "It's uncommon," Chief Sanchez relented. "I see a lotta offspring from wealthy families around here. Usually, they get in some kind of trouble that can be bought away, but still, there's a record, even if it's from their youth. Tony looks to have been an upstanding citizen. Graduated with honors. Never in a lick of trouble. Didn't work much as an adult, but why would he, when he's got a fortune at his disposal?"

"Thank you," Annie nodded, opening the files with an eager turn of the hand. "We'll get to the bottom of this."

Chief Sanchez recognized the dismissal and stood up without offense. She knew that Annie was brilliant, and with brilliance came a certain strangeness that preferred to work alone. "I'll work on smoking out the source of your letter," Chief Sanchez said. "You have my word. A fair trade." With that, she turned the handle on the room's heavy wooden door, letting it click shut behind her.

"What do you think?" Ethan turned to Annie, eager to talk to her now that they were alone.

"I think he was lost," Annie answered, scanning the file on Tony Vasquez. "He didn't know who he was outside of his father's real estate empire."

"I meant about the letter," Ethan added, referencing the mystery of how they'd been hired on their last case. "Can she make headway?"

Annie shrugged, trying not to allow her emotions to betray her. "One case at a time," she said, eyes unmoving. At Ethan's silence, Annie finally looked up. She reached out and placed her hand over his. "Ethan, I *know* Chief Sanchez. She's strategic. If anyone can get us an answer without tipping off the enemy, it's her."

"We could finally bring them justice," Ethan whispered, thinking of Annie's brother and his own sister. It had been years since Ethan had looked at a picture of his sister, and yet, he remembered her face with striking clarity.

"We might," Annie agreed. "But first, I have to do right by Tony Vasquez."

"Fair enough," Ethan said, a resigned edge to his voice. "What are the facts of the case?"

"Tony Vasquez fell from the balcony of his elevent-floor apartment at eight p.m., Pacific Standard Time," Annie began, reading from the open file in front of her. "Police originally expected a suicide, but after an initial investigation, purport foul play due to additional evidence."

"In the form of Ferdinand Vasquez's insistence?" Ethan asked. "That," Annie nodded, "—and this."

She removed a photo from the file, laying it flat in front of Ethan. It depicted a single piece of rope hanging off the edge of the balcony. It looked to be around three feet long and was tied firmly to the balcony's iron railing, the rest of its tail left to hang down toward the Earth.

"They tied him to the railing?" Ethan gasped.

"Appears so. Matching fragments were found on the sleeves of the victim's jacket."

"So they tied him to the railing by the wrists and let him dangle there," Ethan confirmed. "Sounds like cartel behavior. We see it all the time when we're working with drug cases."

"It does look that way," Annie agreed, returning to the paper in front of her. "Tony Vasquez was tied to the railing of his balcony and pushed over the side, and I suspect they allowed Tony's body weight to rip the rope until it separated and he fell."

"If you wanted to kill someone outright, wouldn't you just push them over the edge?" Etha asked. "This looks like a threat gone wrong, or a bid for information. They thought they'd scare it out of him."

"And ended up killing him instead. I suspect the same, but—"

"— suspicions aren't facts," Ethan said, smiling at her. "Let's keep moving with what we know, then."

"We *know* that the building has had a recent problem with suspicious packages arriving that do not list a specific recipient or apartment number. The mailroom has been broken into multiple times in the evening when the head of security is typically off-duty. They even recorded a figure on video but were unable to make a positive I.D. given that the perpetrator covered their face."

"Was it ongoing at the time of the murder?" Ethan asked.

"According to Albert O'Hara, *Rowling Height's* head of security, the issue had resolved altogether in the two months preceding the murder," Annie said. "He attributes this to the fact that he locked the door to the roof, blocking all access."

"The roof?" Ethan said, surprised. "What did that have to do with the packages?"

"Security footage showed the unidentified figure rolling the packages to the roof, where they were presumably stored for some period of time. Once the nightcrawler lost access to the space, the deliveries ceased. Took them awhile to realize he'd been storing the packages there, as they didn't originally have security cameras on the roof or in the corresponding stairwell access. The closest camera was outside the building's gym."

"Interesting," Ethan nodded. "Anything else?"

"Yes, one helpful bit of information," Annie grinned as if she were offering him a present. "The elevator works on key card access only."

"And every resident has a card?"

"Yes," Annie nodded. "They do. To operate the elevator, the resident or employee must scan their card and select a floor. The card company records the time of the swipes, which means we have an access log showing us exactly *who* went to the eleventh floor of the building in the hours before Tony Vasquez was murdered."

She passed a list across the table, letting Ethan scan the names on its surface.

"Looks like we have some suspects," Ethan nodded.

"It's a good place to start," Annie agreed. "Think we should get them together?"

"It might be nice," Ethan said. "After all... it's important to know one's neighbors."

CHAPTER NINE

CATALINE

THE MORNING after the murder had seemed— to Cataline— like one long, painful extension of the evening before. She had managed to sneak in a few hours of sleep, but then, her alarm had gone off at 5 a.m., and she'd awoken with her mind still occupied by the events of the prior evening.

You should tell the police, Cataline thought to herself as she dressed in her small bathroom, a shirt in one hand and a toothbrush in another. Cataline was a person who preferred to do the right thing in every instance. Keeping silent about what she knew went against the core of her being.

After sliding into a simple pair of jeans and a blazer, Cataline crept across the hallway and opened the door to Mario's room. He was still asleep, wrapped up in a Star Wars comforter, his legs hanging over the edge of his bed. Piles of clothes littered the floor, and Cataline said a secret, silent apology to whatever roommates he might live with in the future. She had tried her best to teach Mario to pick up after himself, but it was a losing battle.

Sure that Mario was safe, Cataline stopped at a hanging wall mirror near the front door and adjusted her tie, then slipped out, locking the handle behind her. She marched down the hall to the elevators and scanned her keycard, watching as the buttons came to life with a red glow.

Cataline had been informed that Ferdinand— her boss— had convinced the police to hire a special detective, who would be coming today to question a certain, specific list of suspects. As she pushed the lobby button, Cataline wondered who would be on the list, and if any of them might be residents.

The elevators landed with a ding, and the double doors opened to *Rowling Height's* ornate, stable lobby. Cataline took in the beauty of glistening floors and the gold-laden walls. She had thought of leaving just a mere six months ago, and now, she wished she had. But the building's glittering entryway never failed to remind her why she had stayed. When she came to this country, this was the life she had dreamed of having. It was the life Mario deserved.

Cataline's heels clicked on the floors as she traced a path down a narrow hallway, stopping at a coffee shop that had been allowed to operate out of one of the open commercial spaces. There, she spotted a sight for sore eyes.

"Alfred," Cataline said, his name almost an exhale in her mouth. Alfred was sitting at a marble table, two hot teas and croissants in front of him. Alfred and Cataline had been working together long enough that he knew her order. They had a strong connection and almost never fought. Cataline knew the reason they got along so well was that they both shared a loyalty to the building and a reverence for the positions they were in. Cataline and Alfred genuinely wanted to make *Rowling Heights* the city's ideal living situation. And— until last night— Cataline thought they had come close.

"Have a seat," Alfred motioned at the chair across from him. "We've missed the morning rush again." He motioned around the empty shop. This was their private joke. Each morning, Cataline and Alfred were awake by five or six o'clock, while the rest of the world was still deciding what to do with themselves. Cataline appreciated the way Albert's presence soothed the feeling, turning what could have been a lonely experience into something that felt like a grade-school adventure.

"We have the place to ourselves," Cataline said to him like she always did. She pulled out the chair and took a seat, breaking her croissant half. "You don't think he jumped, do you?"

Albert understood at once she was referring to Tony and shook his head in response. "Certainly not," he said. "Who jumps when they live in a place like this, serviced by such kind people?" He motioned between himself and Cataline. He paused, taking a thoughtful sip of his tea. "There will be an investigation, then?"

"Yes," Cataline said. "They've already compiled a list of suspects. They'll be coming to interview everyone today. Alfred—" She allowed her voice to lower to nothing more than a whisper. "They used the key card data to determine who came and went in the hallway before Tony fell. It's a violation of privacy. When we put that system in I never expected—"

"Nor did I," Alfred said, shaking his head. "And that brings me to my next point." He hesitated, hating to do or say anything that might bring Cataline pain. Still, he knew it was now or never. It would be better to inform her early on before the investigation was deep in process so that she could decide what she needed to do. "There was something that came up on the security footage last night."

"What?" Cataline asked, alarmed.

"It was a few hours before Tony fell," Alfred hedged.

"What did you see?" Cataline asked. Alfred was about to answer but then thought better of it. He presumed they were alone, but there was always the risk of a waiter in the back hearing their mutterings across the shop. Instead, he pulled the square cocktail napkin out from underneath his cup of tea and rummaged through his coat pocket for a pen. He clicked the pen's end and scribbled something on the napkin's doily surface, folding it in half over itself.

"I saw someone on the security tape standing outside Tony's door last night, present in the hallway just hours before Tony was killed."

"Who?" Cataline asked.

Alfred slid the folded napkin across the table. Cataline took it, her heart pounding as she unfolded it in the slightest amount necessary to allow her to read the word within. The blood rushed from her face as she read what was written, there.

"That can't—"

"It was," Alfred interrupted. "Don't worry. I've already deleted the tape. But I thought you should know, in case there's anything that needs to be done about it."

The room seemed to spin as Alfred's words echoed in her ears. There was absolutely something that needed to be done about it. But not now. Not while they were under a microscope.

Cataline reached across the table and touched Alfred's hand. "Thank you," she said. "You're a true friend."

Alfred nodded. It was in his nature to look out for those he cared about. Especially when he suspected they might have gotten themselves into the kind of trouble that could shake the foundations of the finest building— even one as mighty as *Rowling Heights*.

CHAPTER TEN

ANNIE AND ETHAN stood outside an ornate door, its surface carved with flowers. The mansion before them was covered in ivy that weaved its way up the home's brick exterior. For a house belonging to a real estate magnate, the structure lacked any hint of contemporary utilitarianism. The house was warm. It wasn't what Annie had expected, and she hated to be surprised.

"You ring it," Ethan said to Annie, nodding at the doorbell. He hated this part of the job. Meeting the relatives of a victim meant hearing their stories, which reminded Ethan too much of his own tragedies. "Poor guy is probably destroyed," Ethan added, shuffling his feet underneath him.

Annie reached up to push the doorbell but soon discovered there was no need. The door swung open before she could announce her presence, revealing a tall man with broad shoulders and slicked-back hair. He was wearing a black suit, accented by a sharp, checkered tie.

"We're here to see—" Annie started to say.

"Me," Ferdinand Vasquez answered. The edge to his voice said he was a man who preferred to cut right to the chase.

"You're Ferdinand Vasquez?" Ethan confirmed, unable to keep the shock out of his voice.

Ferdinand clocked Ethan's surprised expression. "Didn't live up to your expectations?"

"No, of course not, sir," Ethan stammered. As an FBI agent, it was rare for Ethan to feel rattled. He was used to dealing with all manner of interesting personalities. But something about Ferdinand Vasquez made the people he met feel off-kilter. "It's just— your son died yesterday. I was expecting—"

"That I'd be in bed, inconsolable?" Ferdinand stepped forward, straightening his tie. "Let me tell you a story. I came to this country fleeing communism, on a raft the size of a bicycle. When I touched these shores, I promised myself I would *survive*. And I taught my son to do the same. And the key to survival is *purpose*. When my son was alive, my purpose was making sure he had the best life possible. That he had access to everything I didn't. And now that he's—" Ferdinand's voice broke, and he looked up at the sky, as if hoping he'd find answers there. "—Now that he's gone, my purpose is avenging his death. I want to see the person who did this brought to justice. My son was a survivor, just like me, and he never would have jumped. This was murder. And I intend to see the person responsible behind bars."

"I agree with you," Annie said. "This wasn't a suicide. Your son was murdered."

"You're the one they told me is the genius?" Ferdinand asked, scanning Annie's form from top to bottom, as if looking for any sign of instability.

"Genius is difficult to define," Annie hedged. "But I like to think of it as a special talent in a specific area. In this? I'm the best."

Ferdinand nodded, then opened the door, ushering them into the hallway. "Then we must waste no time," he said, allowing Annie and Ethan into the vast entryway of his enormous, empty home.

———

Mere moments later, Annie and Ethan were seated at Ferdinand's dining room table, a member of his serving staff pouring them two cups of coffee. Crystal kitchenware decorated the solid mahogany surface, delicate glasses and tumblers arranged as a centerpiece that might break with any incorrect movement. Floor to ceiling windows offered a hint of the harbor in the distance, its blue edges barely visible over the top of the fence that enclosed a large backyard.

"It was my first building, and my finest," Ferdinand said, serving himself a pastry off the tray that had been left before them. "*Rowling Heights* has always been special to me because it marked my true transition from one who borrows to one who lends. I wanted my son to have the best, and so, he took the penthouse unit."

"But he didn't work for you, correct? The building has a manager?" Annie asked, pulling a file out of her briefcase and flipping to the appropriate page. Annie had already memorized the facts of the case, but she had learned long ago that pretending to reference information made other people feel more comfortable around her and thus more likely to open up. She pretended to read off the file in front of her. "A miss Cataline?"

"Yes," Ferdinand confirmed. "Cataline handles all the details at *Rowling Heights*. Beneath her as support is my long-time confidant, Alfred. They are both to be trusted."

"Sir, with all due respect, why wouldn't you have your son manage the building?"

Ferdinand laughed as if Annie had told him a joke. "My dear, don't you know where true wealth comes from?" He wiped his face with the edge of his napkin, removing the crumbs that had gathered there. "True wealth doesn't come from work. It comes from *investment.* I encouraged my son to look for places to park his money that would yield more money. I never expected him to waste his time attempting to generate wealth with labor. The rich make money from appropriate placement of funds. If you invest wisely, someone else will work hard for you, and make your money grow many hundreds of times over. *Comprender?"*

"So Tony was an investor?" Ethan asked.

"Tony was training to become as much," Ferdinand said. "He'd made some good bets, and some bad. But he had an eye for opportunity. He could have been great, if only, he'd been given more time—" Ferdinand's voice trailed off, his eyes swelling as if he ached on his son's behalf.

"You told Chief Sanchez you believe something connected to the building led to Tony's death," Annie pushed on, determined to get to the facts. "What did you mean by that? You know the building better than anyone. You can help point us in the right direction. What are we looking for?"

Ferdinand pushed his plate aside. He placed his elbows on the table in front of him, his posture giving the impression of a court judge talking to a defendant. "You'd think an expensive building might buy safety, and in some ways, it does. Where I grew up in Venezuela, we had no street lights, no door locks, and no defense against those who wished to do us harm but our own two hands," Ferdinand held his hands in the air as if to offer an example. "At *Rowling Heights,* we do not see this sort of violence. There are security cameras. There is a sense of protection from the outside world. But it is what lies within that presents a danger. The rich do not fight like the poor. The fight not with fists, but with money."

"Was there someone in the building you believe was out to get your son?" Ethan asked.

"Yes. Whether they were *in* the building I cannot say, but

they certainly wanted to be. In the past month," Ferdinand responded, "I received no less than three offers to rent his apartment at above market rate. They offered to pay the current tenant to vacate the premises, and promised to pay *me* many times the monthly rate."

"Is that unusual, given the fact it's a desirable building and the penthouse unit?" Annie asked.

"It was very unusual," Ferdinand said. "Inquiries and offers we receive are generally only for apartments currently listed on the market for rent. What was even stranger was that the offers were made directly to my lawyers from an anonymous source. The source claimed to be an international billionaire who preferred to remain unnamed. I rejected the offer each time it was presented, and with each rejection, the presumptive rate increased. Answer me this, Detective Annie Hudson. Why would a billionaire, with all the resources in the world, continue to push to lease that exact unit in our building?"

"I don't know," Annie answered truthfully. "But I agree with you. It's suspicious."

"And you believe it's connected to someone currently living in the building?" Ethan asked.

Ferdinand nodded. "The unit was of course not listed for rent, as I had already given it Tony. So, I must ask, how did the anonymous buyer even know the penthouse unit existed? And why would they be willing to pay so much more than market rate for a unit they'd never seen?"

Annie and Ethan exchanged a glance. It was a fair question.

"And there was something else," Ferdinand leaned in, momentarily resting his head in his hands. He pulled at his hair as if what he was about to say made him wish he could escape himself. "In the paperwork, they included a statement offering to pay the current tenant to move. But they made a mistake. I thought nothing of it at the time, but they did not simply say "the current tenant." No... instead, they addressed Tony— as my *son*." The word seemed to hurt as it escaped Ferdinand's lips. "They knew my *son* was living there. How could a foreign investor know such a thing? We are a very private people. For our safety, we ensure our information is not available online. Given my wealth, we take extraordinary precautions. They could not have known unless—"

"Unless they'd met Tony themselves," Annie concluded.

"They must have known us, either through the building or through our closest social sphere. I wish now that I had accepted their offer," Ferdinand said, for the first time looking as if he might crumble. "My son would still have his future. All of this, for a penthouse? I own thirty penthouses. And only one son."

Annie reached across the table and put her hand over Ferdinand's. "Thank you, sir. For what it's worth, I don't think you're wrong." She retracted her hand, and Ferdinand looked up at her, glad, for once, to be believed. "I think someone in the building is absolutely behind this. Our next move is to speak to the residents. I promise you— we'll get the answers you're looking for."

With that, Annie stood, indicating it was time for them to take their leave. Ferdinand escorted them back into the foyer, grateful, but afraid to hope that justice might be served.

"Be careful," Ferdinand said as he opened the front door for his guests. "Remember what I've said. The rich do not fight their battles with hands and fists but with loyalty. Determine where those two things lie, and you'll find my answers. The people in this building— they build connections with each other. Alliances. They will go where their loyalty is and lie for the ones that benefit them. Determine who they have tied themselves to and you will know where their interests lie."

"Sir, if you don't mind me asking," Annie probed. "Where does your loyalty lie?"

"With my son," Ferdinand said, the heartbreak in his eyes apparent. "For him, I do everything." He motioned to the suit he was wearing. "Even now, I get dressed in the morning because it's what he would have expected from me."

"Thank you again for your time," Annie said. They descended down the steps, the bright, morning air surrounding them once again. After talking to Ferdinand, the beauty of the day seemed almost insulting given the depth of his pain.

"The suit looks nice on you," Ethan called back to Ferdinand, his voice soft as he turned his head over his shoulder, taking one more look at one of the city's wealthiest men who had suddenly found himself impoverished in the way that mattered most to him.

CHAPTER ELEVEN

ROWLING HEIGHT'S modern lobby was busy today. Residents, guests, and shoppers scurried across the marble atrium, many of them holding coffees and newspapers. Cataline stood in the middle of the bustle, still as a statue. Nobody gave her a second glance or wondered at the stationary woman frozen in the lobby. Cataline was used to being ignored when she was in uniform. Today, invisibility was the least of her problems.

Cataline broke the spell of stillness with a lift of her left arm, turning her wristwatch toward her face to view the time. If her guests were punctual, they'd be arriving any minute now.

Like clockwork, Annie and Ethan appeared at the lobby doors. They locked eyes with her at once, and Cataline forced a smile onto her face, waving from across the room. She strode towards them, trying to pretend this was simply an ordinary day, and that these were two very ordinary guests.

"You must be Annie Hudson," Cataline said, reaching out to shake Annie's hand. "*Bienvenida*. I saw the special feature they did on you for 20/20. Prior crime victim dedicates life to solving murders. What a resume you have."

Annie shrugged, lifting a pair of sunglasses off her eyes. "Ethan made me do it. Said it would help him market my services to the agency."

Next to Annie, Ethan held out his hand. "Ethan Beckett," he offered. "FBI Agent. But my most important role is being Annie Hudson's sidekick."

"*Afortunada*," Cataline couldn't help but mutter. *Lucky.* The word slipped out before she had a chance to sensor herself. She couldn't help but notice that Ethan was attractive. Not in a movie star way, but in the kind of grounded, imperfect fashion that made a woman think he could be depended on. Cataline cleared her throat. "I've booked one of our meeting spaces. If you'll just follow me..." Cataline motioned for Annie and Ethan to follow her down an enormous hallway to the right of the foyer's entrance.

"This looks like much more than an apartment building," Annie nodded at the coffee shop as they passed. Beside the shop sat two other stores. The first sold island-themed vacation clothing, demonstrated on a mannequin displayed by the entryway, his plastic body covered by a Hawaiian shirt and pair of khaki pants. The second store was a pharmacy, a red medic's cross decorating the front counter, racks of painkillers, toilet paper, and beauty products sprawling across the remainder of the floor space.

"The original concept was a live-work environment, but Ferdinand ultimately decided to settle for apartments up top and stores down below," Cataline said as they turned the corner. "His vision for *Rowling Heights* was that a resident could meet almost every need they had without ever leaving the building. We have a coffee shop, and some retail space... upstairs there's a gym and an indoor pool. It's a fantastic place to live. We attend to every concern."

"Except for being thrown off balconies," Ethan said.

"Yes," Cataline cringed. "Except for that one." She paused.

"Tony was a friend," she added. "If there were anything all of us could have done, we would have—"

"Of course you would have," Annie said, shooting Ethan a sideways glance. "This wasn't your fault. We're going to get to the bottom of it."

"Apologies," Ethan added. "It was a bad joke. Being in the Bureau means you see it all. We laugh about it to function. Sometimes I forget to leave it back with the FBI."

"That's alright," Cataline said, stopping at the entrance to a conference room. A plaque outside the door read, "*Eastern Wing.*" "This is our best conference room. I've invited every resident on the list you sent."

"Was there anyone who refused to attend?" Annie asked.

"No one. They all agreed to come. Like I said, we loved Tony. He wasn't just the landlord's son. He was one of us." Cataline paused, straightening her tie. "All the residents should be present. If someone is missing, feel free to give me a call. Otherwise, I have some business to attend to on the ninth floor—"

"Oh!" Annie exclaimed, covering her mouth as if a horrible mistake had been made. "I'm so sorry, I should have been clearer."

"Excuse me?" Cataline asked, taken aback.

"Your name was on the list too," Annie added. "It was first on the list, actually."

Cataline's heart pounded. Beneath the tightly woven threads of her suit jacket, a bead of sweat dripped down the side of her arm. She swallowed hard, then forced another smile, doing her best to hide the absolute terror that coursed through her veins. "I assumed you were simply addressing it to me—"

"No," Annie confirmed. "I had hoped you would stay. What you have to say about that night could be really helpful for us." Annie smiled at Cataline as if she were asking her to an afternoon tea. "Unless, of course, there's a problem?"

"No," Cataline shook her head. "No problem at all."

With that, Cataline followed Annie and Ethan into the conference room, thinking about what she had to lose if this meeting didn't end in her favor.

———

Minutes later, and the meeting was off to a rocky start. The conference room at *Rowling Heights* was a trim space with a contained, elaborate charm. A flat carpet with printed pink flowers ran the span of the room, and foldable wooden chairs had been arranged in a line. Mirrors on the ceiling gave the impression the space could be used in case of a ball, and ornate light fixtures on the wall cast a golden glow about the windowless room. Against the far wall, a table had been set up to provide a continental breakfast, bagels, fruit, and a coffeemaker offering an advance apology to all who had given their time to the event this morning.

The residents of *Rowling Heights* shuffled in their seats, each of them trying hard not to look at each other. Half-eaten bagels and plates of fruits balanced on their knees. Cataline had selected a place at the end of the line of chairs, next to Alfred, who was sipping coffee from a paper mug. He nodded his head at her in a subtle acknowledgment but didn't dare say more.

In front of the line of chairs, Annie and Ethan stood side-by-side, doing their best to appear as if they came in peace.

"Thank you all for coming today," Annie said to the residents. "I won't take too much of your time." A quick scan of the faces present told her that nobody believed her.

"We'd like to attach some faces to names," Ethan said, glancing down at a list on a clipboard in front of him. "When I call your name, please raise a hand." Ethan cleared his throat. The truth was, Annie and Ethan had run a complete background check on every resident that appeared on the list late last night, and they knew not only what each person looked like, but their credit history and social security number. Still, Annie had insisted he go through the farce of taking a roll call. She said it had something to do with creating a sense of spontaneity in which each suspect would let down their guard. The exercise, she claimed, would give her the opportunity to observe behavior.

"Cataline, of course," Ethan smiled at Cataline, who immediately raised her hand. She attempted to keep her expression even, as if this were just another day at the office.

"Alfred O'Hara?" Ethan asked, looking around the room as if he had no idea where Alfred was. Next to Cataline, Alfred lifted a hand in the air. He was pale and greying, plump in a way that suggested good health and a lack of wanting. His uniform was ironed, stiffened so it lay perfectly in place. Annie noted the care with which Alfred treated his uniform. It told her that he valued his position here at *Rowling Heights*.

"Mindy Wellington?" In the middle of the room, Mindy's arm floated upwards, her face impossible to read. Her jaw was set tight, a dimple forming in the middle of her cheek. Her hair was cut in a flattering, blunt style, and she gave the impression of being rather ageless despite being a woman in her 50s.

"Hathaway Wellington?" Ethan said, again scanning the room. Five chairs down from Mindy, Hathaway thrust a hand up, then pulled it back down as quickly as he had raised it. His shirt was buttoned unevenly, and the grey beard that grew on his chin was coming in unevenly.

"Are you two related?" Annie joked. She knew from her research, of course, that they were in the process of a divorce, but she wanted to see what both of them would do when prodded.

"We used to be married, but now we're separated," Mindy said, keeping her tone even.

"We're *still* married," Hathaway corrected her.

"Nobody asked you to clarify—"

"Well maybe they should of, considering *you* got it wrong."

"What am I supposed to say?" Mindy added. "We're separated but still legally married so although we can barely stand to be in the same room together, yes, there is a vague legal connection that prolongs our mutual pain?"

There was a long pause.

"That would have been better," Hathaway said.

"Alejandro?" Ethan broke the silence as if nothing had happened. A hand on the far left of the row of chairs appeared in the air. Bracelets dangled from its wrist, expensive gold and silver layers donning the skin of the owner. Alejandro flashed a too-white smile, popping the collar on his silk, paisley shirt. "That's me," he confirmed. "*Gracias, hombre guapo.*" He winked at Ethan.

Annie couldn't help but think that Alejandro reminded her of a *tella novella* star— plastic in a way that was almost too perfect.

"Thanks," Ethan nodded. "And last up... Montana Grant?"

The final hand in the room raised. A sleeve of tattoos covered the corresponding arm, landing at the shoulder of a broad man with pock-marked skin. "That's me," Montana said, not seeming to care too much whether he was present or not. Annie noticed the way Cataline glanced at him. She let her eyes rest on his frame for only a moment before looking away again, a sharp inhale rattling her chest. It could have been a meaningless glance, and Annie didn't know what to make of it. But she filed the acknowledgement away in her brilliant mind, saving it for later use.

"That's everyone," Annie acknowledged, stepping forward to face the group. She opened her arms wide like a presenter at a conference, welcoming them into what she was about to say. "First, I want to thank you all for being here. I should reiterate what I'm sure Cataline told you, which is that your attendance is not legally required at this meeting. It's merely an opportunity for you to share what you know about the night Tony Vasquez died."

"But anything we say can be used as evidence," Hathaway spoke up, still rooted to his chair. He looked rather pleased with himself that he'd contributed something useful. Further down the line of seats, Mindy resisted the urge to roll her eyes.

"That's true," Annie said. "Anything you say can be used against you in a court of law, and you have the right to request the services of an attorney, or to not speak it all. Now, with that out of the way," she clapped her hands together with an excitement that said she was about to attend the world's great party. "Let's begin. As all of you know by now, Tony Vasquez fell from the floor of his penthouse apartment, landing on a sedan parked down below. He was killed immediately on impact."

"It wasn't suicide," Alfred stated with confidence, rubbing his chin. His eyes were flooded with a deep concern that made his irises shift from grey-blue to sea-green. "No one in this building has much to be unhappy about. He couldn't have felt that low. We would have noticed."

"I'm sure you would have," Annie agreed. "No, we do not believe this was a suicide."

"Based on what evidence?" Montana asked, adjusting the pant leg of his jeans. He tucked the denim deeper into the cavern of his cowboy boot, resting his heel back on the ground with satisfaction. "People kill themselves all the time. No reason to leap to murder."

Annie reached into her briefcase and removed a printed photograph. The air in the room seemed to thicken as the residents of *Rowling Heights* leaned in to get a better look. The photograph was an image of Tony's balcony taken from the outside. Based on the angle, the image had to have been captured by a drone, given that it would have been impossible for any human to suspend themselves in mid-air at such a height. The photograph showed the top three stories of *Rowling Heights*, with Tony's penthouse balcony taking up the upper third of the page. There— across iron grating that provided a shield against accidental slips toward death— was the offending object.

"Pretty clear when you see it like this, isn't it?" Annie asked. She pointed to the item in question as if the photograph were a game of *Where's Waldo*. There, at the end of her finger, was the undeniable shape of a rope. When compared to the massive scale of the apartment building, the rope looked to be about three feet long, its edges frayed and hanging down toward the balcony below Tony Vasquez's apartment. It was an ominous, strikingly simple last call— an epitaph to Tony, left for the world to see.

"Take it away," Alejandro said, looking rather pale. "It's disgusting to see such a thing at our home. *Me da nauseas.*"

Annie obliged and removed the picture from view, slipping it back into her briefcase. "As you can see, this was a murder. Tony Vasquez didn't fall off his balcony, and he didn't jump," she paused for dramatic effect. "He was pushed."

Mindy raised her hand. Annie nodded at her, and she pulled her fur-trimmed cardigan tighter around her shoulders. "Not to be rude but, what does this have to do with any of us? A hundred people live here. You could have had the whole building come to this meeting. Why us?"

Annie smiled, glad that Mindy had given her the perfect opening to discuss the topic she was most interested in exploring. "Excellent question," Annie said. "You all are here because the keycards used to access the elevator record the movements of all residents."

Surprised glances swept across the room. Albert appeared to blush, looking at a sconce on the wall to avoid eye contact with any of the residents. Annie was pleased to see they seemed not to have been aware of the key cards function beyond operating the elevator.

"According to the records provided by the company that provides the cards, every one of you is the registered owner of a card that was used to access the eleventh floor within the twenty-four hour period preceding Tony's demise. And of course, besides the gym and the indoor pool, the only unit on the eleventh floor is—"

"The Penthouse," Cataline said under her breath, completing Annie's sentence without even meaning to say a single a word.

The residents stared at each other, shocked expressions showing none of them had expected this news. In a subtle gesture, Mindy pushed her chair away from her neighbors, as if she no longer wanted to be associated with them. Hathaway gripped the edge of his seat, thinking about his tropical fish and pretending he was anywhere else but sitting in the conference room. Montana appeared unphased, glancing at his nails and picking at some dirt that hid underneath. Alfred and Cataline shared a sideways glance with one another, both of them thinking that resident complaints were sure to skyrocket in response to this development.

It was Alejandro who finally broke the silence, rolling up the sleeves on his silk shirt. "This is excellent news, that you have such strong leads!" He plastered a smile on his face. "I'm sure we'd all be happy to help. I know half the police department if it would assist you. I can make a call—"

"That won't be necessary," Annie said, making a note to herself. Alejandro was a networker, and slippery. This would need to be explored. But not now. Today, there was only one piece of information Annie needed to help her narrow down the suspects. "You all would be a great help if you could answer one simple question." She paused, scanning the group for reactions. "Why did you visit the eleventh floor in the twenty-four hours before Tony died?"

At first, nobody volunteered to share an alibi, but then, Montana spoke up. "The gym," he shrugged, his voice a gentle huff. "It's on the eleventh floor, at the other end of the hallway from the penthouse."

"Is that correct?" Annie asked Alfred. He nodded.

"The gym and the penthouse are the only amenities on the eleventh floor, besides the penthouse. "

"Do you go to the gym often?" Annie turned back to Montana.

"I'm DHS," Montana said in response. He reached into his shirt pocket and pulled out a black bifold wallet, allowing it to fall open to reveal a badge. "Department of Homeland Security." He closed the wallet, tucking it back in his pocket. "Lotta tough situations I get into. Gotta stay in shape. Probably the same as you," he nodded at Agent Ethan Beckett, who offered little in return. "It's part of my job," Montana added. "They expect it."

"Did you see anything while you were there? Anything out of the ordinary?"

"No," Montana said. "I went in. Did some lifts. Got out. Nothing out of the ordinary. Sorry."

"Anyone else?" Annie asked, waiting for another volunteer. Across the row of chairs, Hathaway raised his hand.

"I pressed the wrong button," he said, looking embarrassed. "I'm sorry?"

"I live on the tenth floor," Hathaway elaborated. "I got in the elevator to go home after a long day. I was on the phone having an, uh, *conversation* with my lawyer—" Hathaway couldn't help but glance at Mindy. "I thought I hit the button for floor ten. But turns out, I hit eleven. The elevator landed. The doors opened. I stepped out and wrapped up my call. As soon as I hung up I realized at once I was in the wrong hallway. Then I turned right around, got back in and went home."

"How long did it take to get back in the elevator?"

"No more than five minutes," Hathaway shrugged. "I was quite carried away on the call. You might even say I was yelling." Hathaway looked at the ground, shame making wrinkles at the edges of his eyes. "It was a rather emotional call. You see, my wife and I are getting a divorce."

"*Ex*-wife," Mindy muttered.

"It's not 'ex' until the divorce is final, which it *would* be if you would only agree to honor the prenup you *already signed—*"

"Here we go again! " Mindy said to him, her voice an octave higher than it had been just moments ago. "Always diminishing my contributions!"

"By asking you to honor what you agreed to?" Hathaway countered.

"What I agreed when I was young and stupid enough to bet on *you—*"

"Thank you," Annie interrupted. "What about you?" She was looking at Mindy. "Why did you go to the eleventh floor?"

Mindy's expression was flat with surprise, almost as if Annie had asked to see her underwear. "Me?" She looked around, suddenly regretting that she'd drawn so much attention to herself by engaging with her ex-husband.

"Yes," Annie said.

"Well, I—" Mindy paused, thinking. "I was following *him*," she nodded at Hathaway. "I heard him on the phone with his lawyer and I thought I'd get a jump on what they were strategizing."

"You low-down dirty—" Hathaway sputtered.

"As if you wouldn't do the exact same!" Mindy shouted.

"Excellent," Annie nodded. "Anyone else care to volunteer why they visited the penthouse floor.

"Business," Alejandro said, popping his shirt collar. "I run multiple businesses, and Tony was interested in investing. Did you know I own the largest Tequila business in San Diego? Maybe even the West Coast? *Es muy grande*," Alejandro added with a glint in his eye.

"I was unaware," Annie said.

"Tony wanted to invest in my next venture, but I told him I didn't think he'd be a good fit. My investors are an exclusive group. Russian money. Saudi oil. Tony would have been the odd man out."

"I see," Annie nodded, pretending to be impressed. "So you went to break the news to Tony?"

"I did," Alejandro grimaced. "I stopped by. Told him it wasn't going to work out and he couldn't invest with us. He seemed upset. When we all thought it was a suicide I worried that was why he..." Tony made a whistling sound and indicated a person jumping with his pointer finger. "So I'm happy to hear it was a murder. Because this, of course, means it wasn't my fault."

"Yes," Annie shook her head in disbelief. "What a relief." She scanned the room, turning to the only two suspects who hadn't yet spoken. "That's it for residents, which leaves our employees, Alfred and Cataline. Alfred?"

"I was doing a security sweep," Alfred offered. "Every night before I'm off the clock to head home, I walk the halls and make sure everything's in order. I stop by every floor. Not just the eleventh."

"Did you see anything unusual that evening?"

"No. It was quiet. The doors to the roof were still sealed. I'd been checking them since the package disaster—"

"The roof access is on the eleventh floor?" Annie perked up, suddenly interested.

"Well, yes," Alfred added.

"But earlier you said the penthouse and the gym were the only spaces?"

"I misspoke," Alfred said, clearly surprised that Annie didn't miss a thing. "I didn't consider the roof access stairs because, well, they're locked and sealed. No one can use them."

"And you didn't see anything strange that night?'

"Nothing," Alfred confirmed.

Annie nodded, turning to the last remaining victim: Cataline. "Cataline. Why did *you* go to the eleventh floor?"

Cataline inhaled, resisting the urge to reach up and touch the crucifix around her neck. She dug her feet into the ground, biting the inside of her cheek. She grounded herself, promising to appear effortless as she leaned into the lie she knew she had to tell. The lie that would save her and Mario from a terrible fate.

"Cleaning check," Cataline said.

"Was there a reason you suspected the eleventh floor needed a check for cleaning?"

"No," Cataline exhaled, staying focused on the moment. "But I check all the floors in rotation every few weeks. I make sure I stop by personally. If you just take the cleaning crew's word for it, well, I've found that doesn't work out as well."

"And this week just happened to be floor eleven?"

"Just so happened," Cataline confirmed. "Funny timing."

"Very funny," Annie agreed. There was a moment in which Annie opened her mouth as if to say more, but then she stopped, turning instead to the group. "Thank you all again. That's all we need for today. I hope you won't mind if we follow up to conduct individual interviews. Your cooperation is greatly appreciated."

With that, the group rose as one, their bodies elbowing one another toward the exit. Cataline trailed behind, relieved that it appeared the detective had bought her story. The guilt of the lie sat heavy in her chest, the weight of it making her want to lay on the floor. Instead, she walked toward the exit as if nothing had happened, hoping this would be the last of the detective's questions for her.

When the room had cleared out, Ethan sunk into one of the abandoned chairs, his arms spreading wide over its back. "Tough crowd," he said. "What do you think?"

Annie sat down next to him, letting her head fall onto his shoulder. It was a moment that surprised Ethan. Annie didn't usually show affection so easily. He held still as if a butterfly had landed on his arm, afraid to move in case he scared it away.

"I think," Annie said, eyes distant. "It will be great fun to find out why they're all lying."

CHAPTER TWELVE

CATALINE

WHEN THE MEETING with the detectives ended, Cataline tried to go about her ordinary activities supporting the day-to-day operations of *Rowling Heights,* but couldn't shake the feeling she was being watched. She held her afternoon meeting with the cleaning staff, discussing the upkeep of the common areas and the need for better attention to be paid to the hallway near the lobby. She listened with empathetic ears to a resident from the third floor, who felt the garbage disposal in his kitchen sink kept backing up not because he shoved paper towels down the pipe, but because the building needed to upgrade its plumbing system. She offered a tour of a vacant unit on the fifth floor to a prospective tenant, who— based on their description of income and credit— would never qualify to live in the building anyway.

And of course, Cataline fielded multiple requests from Hathaway, who had treated her like his personal assistant since the moment of his separation from Mindy. In the morning, Hathaway called requesting additional toilet paper and paper towels be ordered and delivered to his apartment. In the afternoon, he sent Cataline a text message requesting a list of the best dry-cleaning services in the surrounding area. Hathaway treated the building more like a hotel than an apartment complex, and his requests were so basic Cataline couldn't help but wonder if perhaps he only made them so often because he was lonely. Out of concern for his well-being, she never denied a single "ask" Hathaway made, granting all his wishes whenever she could. Cataline knew what it was like to see one's life turned upside down overnight, and even though he treated her more like a vending machine than a person, Cataline felt sorry for him.

Throughout all the ordinary ups and downs of her day, Cataline couldn't help but glance at the security cameras that hung in every corner, a shiver running down her spine.

When she'd had the cameras installed, Cataline thought it would offer an additional perk to residents— something the team at *Rowling Heights* was always eager to do. Cataline still remembered the day she'd sat down with Alfred, the two of them thinking up low-cost, high-benefit improvements they could make to the property. They'd sat elbow-to-elbow in his closet of an office, eager to spend the small allotment Ferdinand had offered them as a slush fund for upgrades to the building.

"A jacuzzi spa?" Cataline remembered asking, wistful. The building had an indoor pool, but it's proximity to the beach made the pool less appealing in the eyes of many would-be tenants. Still, a jacuzzi was in their budget, and Cataline herself wouldn't have minded the ability to take a soak after a long day on her feet.

Alfred shook his head. "Those bloody things leak. They jam. We'd have to have to tear up the gym."

"Fine, don't let me dream. *Olvídelo!*" Cataline laughed. "It's not about me, anyway," she added. "What would our prospective tenants want?" She paused, trying to see the world through the eyes of their residents. "What does our clientele worry about? What problems do they need solved?"

"Security," Alfred brightened as the idea hit him all at once.

"They're pretty secure on the upper floors," Cataline reasoned. "This is one of the safest buildings in town what with the key cards and the location—"

"It's not about actually being secure," Alfred reasoned. "It's about *feeling* secure. The presence of cameras makes people feel safer. It convinces them there's recourse if their place is robbed. Plus it adds an air of exclusivity. The wealthy like to feel they're getting the best money can buy. A top of the line security system achieves that."

Alfred made his argument, and Cataline was eventually won over, approving the installation of over a dozen cameras spread across every floor on the property. She'd been surprised to see that even the extensive system they'd ordered left blank spaces— areas that weren't able to be observed. It turned out that absolutely security was more difficult to achieve than Claudine had imagined. But the point of the cameras was never actually increasing safety, but rather, escalating the feeling of exclusivity within the building. And the security system seemed to achieve that. Prospective tenants seemed impressed by the idea of someone watching. At the time, the cameras had seemed like a good addition to the building.

But today, after sitting in the group interrogation before the detectives, the idea that someone was watching made Cataline uneasy. Even later in the evening from the safety of her own, unobserved apartment, Cataline was bothered by the feeling.

Now, the day was ending, and Cataline stood over a pot of boiling sauce, clutching a wooden spoon in her hand, turning it in circles as she considered all she had learned.

Ironic, she thought. *Ironic that I approved the installation of the cameras.*

She glanced over her shoulder. Behind her, Mario sat on

the couch, a discarded video game controller on the table in front of him. Mario was working on his homework— an English essay— and would occasionally stop typing on his laptop long enough to look at the controller with longing. He'd been instructed that he could play a game only after homework, and *after* dinner— a space of time that seemed very far away.

Cataline knew she had to have a difficult conversation with her son. All she ever wanted was to pull him closer, which was what made confrontation so painful. Mario was her only family. She hated to do anything that might push him away.

She let the spoon rest on the edge of the pot and turned the heat down low. It was now or never. She had lied to the detectives when she'd given them her alibi for the night Tony Vasquez was killed. Because the truth was, Cataline hadn't gone to the eleventh floor that day. Her keycard— which had unlimited access to every floor— had gone to level where Tony Vasquez was murdered. But it had made the journey with Cataline.

And there was only one person besides Cataline who used her keycard.

Cataline sat on the couch, folding her hands in her lap. Mario glanced up from his essay. He shut his computer, recognized at once the expression on her face.

"Am I in trouble?" he asked.

"Maybe," Cataline admitted. "But if you're honest with me, I think I can help."

Mario gulped. He pushed the computer aside, his hands shaking a little. He was a good kid, who hated conflict as much as his mother. Still, he had been expecting this. The moment came as no surprise. It was hard to keep a secret at *Rowling Heights*.

"I told the Detectives it was me who went to the eleventh floor the night Tony Vasquez was killed," Cataline said.

"You don't think I—" Mario's mouth dropped open in shock. "Of course not."

"Tony was my friend," Mario said, pulling his baseball cap down lower over his eyes. The gesture was familiar to Cataline. It was something Mario had always done when he was upset, as if thought hiding his eyes would conceal his emotion. "We played video games together."

"You can't tell people that now," Cataline added. "Alfred showed me the security tape."

Mario glanced back up at his mother, as if an idea had only just hit him. "So you saw the whole thing?"

"I didn't see it, but Alfred described what happened to me," Cataline said. Alfred had offered her a detailed description of what he'd seen on the security footage before deleting the tape. The video was brief, but damning. It showed Mario, exiting the elevator on the eleventh floor, a hoodie thrown over the baseball cap he wore almost every day. In the tape, Mario had glanced to the right and left, checking both sides of the hallway. Then, he'd run toward Tony's apartment, stopping at the front door. There, in front of Tony Vasquez's apartment, sat a small, brown package. It was wrapped in paper, a simple address label on its exterior. Mario had bent down, picked up the package, and stuffed it inside his sweatshirt before zipping up the jacket and running back to the elevator. Needless to say, the moment had been suspicious.

"They don't think I killed him because of that, do they?" Mario gasped.

"No, because they don't *know*. Your uncle Alfred deleted the tape."

Mario breathed a sigh of relief, but Cataline wasn't about to let him off the hook that easy.

"Mario," Cataline said, an edge to her voice. "Tell me it hasn't been you moving the packages around the building?" Her tone changed octaves as the panic she tried to keep at bay started to flood her mind with images: Mario surrounded by boxes. Mario shipping drugs. Mario going to prison. "You're not involved with something dangerous, are you? You wouldn't keep something like that from me? You know you're not allowed on the roof—"

"Mom!" Mario stopped her. "The packages weren't me. Don't you think you would've heard me leaving all those nights?"

His words brought Cataline back down to Earth.

"This is the first time I've done anything like this. And Tony said I could."

"*Tony* said you could steal his mail?"

"It wasn't stealing," Mario said. "It—" he paused, embarrassed. "I didn't want you to know what I ordered. I worried it might upset you. Tony said I could have it sent to his place instead and pick it up outside his door."

Cataline's eyes darkened. "What did you order?"

"You have to promise not to be mad."

"Mario Julio! *Ya estoy enojada.* I am *already* mad. You show me that package right now. *Vamos!*"

Mario rose from his seat, dragging his feet into his bedroom. He emerged a few moments later with the package in hand, but the paper had been ripped open, the sleeves of the box inside dangling in the air. Mario handed the box to Cataline. She peered inside, taking in air when she saw what lay within. Cataline felt her heart pound against the walls of her chest. She'd known this day would come, but didn't think it would come so soon.

"I needed to know," Mario said, his words tumbling out at a rapid-fire pace. "I love you the most but I thought maybe it would help us. I just needed—"

"Enough," Cataline felt her cheeks flush, rage and terror flooding the tips of her fingers. "You will never do this again. *Comprende?*"

Mario nodded. "But maybe if you just told me—"

"Not tonight," Cataline said, and that was the end of it.

She shoved the box in a kitchen cabinet high above the countertops, far out of Mario's reach. Mario returned to his homework as Cataline attended to the sauce. She hated herself for being so hard on him, but he had no idea what was at stake. Cataline *had* to be hard on Mario, because what he didn't know might kill him. And now, the danger that had once been so far from both of them was right outside their door, living on another floor of *Rowling Heights*.

CHAPTER THIRTEEN

TONY VASQUEZ'S front door was marked by a long, sagging piece of yellow tape that read, "Crime Scene, Do Not Cross." Detective Annie Hudson stepped forward, pulling the tape away from the edge of the frame with a resigned lack of care.

"The key?" Annie turned to Ethan, who shrugged at her.

"The door was unlocked when they got here," he said. "Should be unlocked."

"I'd still like to test it," Annie answered. Ethan nodded, dropping his FBI standard-issue tactical bag on the ground. He sorted through a series of plastic bags within, extracting a single, silver key that had been admitted into evidence. Annie removed the key from its casing and positioned it in front of the lock.

"You'd think if they bothered to use keycards for the elevators, they'd upgrade the whole place," Ethan thought aloud.

"What's stranger is that this lock has been forced," Annie said. She held up the key from her position, crouched under the door handle near the manual lock. "See?" She attempted to force the key into the lock, but it didn't open. "Somebody picked the lock and broke the internal hardware."

"Not very skilled then, were they?"

"Most certainly not," Annie agreed. She pushed the door open and pocketed the key. Ethan followed behind her and the two of them stood for a moment in Tony's elaborate foyer, taking in the grandeur of the Penthouse suite.

The unit had been newly re-modeled in the popular open-concept fashion, with a kitchen that provided an unobstructed view of the sunken living room. A wall-mounted entertainment system featuring an enormous flat-screen television gave the impression of an in-home movie theatre. Across from the entertaining area, floor-to-ceiling windows looked out at the harbor, providing an unobstructed view of the sunset across the bay. Cement floors spanned the entirety of the home, and Tony— or perhaps a clever interior decorator— had laid ornate carpets over the contemporary material to give the space some warmth. The couches were custom-made from the softest leather, fitted exactly to the measurements of the sunken living room. A fireplace was fitted into the wall-to-wall bookshelf that spanned the back half of the unit, giving a sense of endlessness to the biggest room in the penthouse suite. Overhead, a chandelier dangled from the twelve-foot ceilings. Experienced in its entirety, it was an impressive sight.

"The FBI doesn't pay me enough," Ethan opined.

"But they allow you to traipse across the country with me," Annie reminded him.

"That's priceless."

Annie meandered toward the floor-to-ceiling windows, ignoring the grandeur within the apartment and focusing instead on the elements of nature on display outside the glass. The penthouse's view was stunning. In the distance, the San Diego Harbor created a semi-circle around a placid, turquoise ocean. Sails billowed in the wind, and on the Southern side of the harbor, tall skyscrapers reached for the sun, their metal frames a striking, man-made interruption in the otherwise untouched bay. A protective stretch of land separated the harbor from the larger ocean, creating a cove through which a single opening allowed boats to make their way out to sea. On the less developed Northern side, small buildings dotted the landscape, none of them more than three stories high. A pier jutted into the harbor, encircled by a stretch of sandy beach and a cement pedestrian path with a special lane for bike traffic. Closest to the sand, a stucco-covered building asserted its position as having access to its own, private pier. A solid, stone wall prohibited entry, and a series of parked power boats lay in wait behind the barrier. The boats' sides were painted black and white, with "Department of Homeland Security" written on their bellies. They were arranged in such straight, even lines that they looked to Annie like soldiers getting ready for battle. Based on the boats, Annie surmised the firm, square building behind them belonged to DHS as well. Next to it all, at the end of the Northern stretch of land, an imposing lighthouse teetered at the edge of the sea.

"Quite the view, isn't it?" Ethan asked over Annie's shoulder.

"Yes, it is," she agreed. "What do you make of this?" Annie pointed to a construction site across the street. It was to the right of the field of view through Tony's window and was still a work in progress, its steel beams exposed to the elements. It looked to be about ten stories tall, and partially obscured the view of the Northern part of the harbor. If not for the fact the penthouse was on the eleventh floor, it would have blocked the view entirely.

"It's sad for the other residents, isn't it?" Ethan answered. "To pay to live in a place like this only to see the view obscured. But no skin off Tony's back. He could still see everything from here."

"Yes, he could," Annie agreed, looking again at those DHS boats, all of them poised to leap into action at any moment. "He could see everything."

"Is that important?" Ethan wondered aloud.

"I think it might be."

Ethan couldn't help but allow his surprise to show on his face. Annie was a closed book, rarely allowing him into her process during an investigation. He couldn't help but wonder if she was finally letting her guard down. The two of them had moved closer during their last investigation, and he hoped to keep heading in that direction.

"It's just a hunch," Annie smiled at him as if she were reading his thoughts. "Should we get on with the dirty?"

"My favorite part," Ethan agreed. He dropped his bag and pulled out two pairs of latex gloves, passing one set to Annie. They pulled on the protective devices, eager to explore without contaminating the crime scene.

"We'll start with the kitchen?"

Ethan followed Annie into the open-concept kitchen, noting the Viking appliances and double-door fridge. He opened what looked like an ordinary drawer, only to find a dishwasher hidden behind it. Further down the line of appliances, opening a pantry door revealed a walk-in butler's cabinet with space for dry food storage.

"I would fill this all with instant noodles, too," Ethan said, noting that multiple shelves had been dedicated to instant packaged ramen. "Shame to waste a kitchen like this on a guy who couldn't cook."

"Looks like he could drink, though," Annie nodded at three bottom shelves in the pantry, which featured lines of tequila bottles. "Isn't it strange it's all the same brand?" Annie leaned in, reading the labels. "La Vida Liquors. Have you heard of it?"

"Never. But I'm more of a whiskey guy."

"There's nothing else. No other alcohol. Just the Tequila,"

Annie thought aloud. "Who buys thirty bottles of the same brand of tequila, but not something else to mix it with?"

"Unusual," Ethan agreed.

"He was lonely," Annie said. "All the money in the world and no one to share it with."

Annie snapped a photo of the bottles on her phone, then floated back into the space by the windows. Ethan trailed behind her as if she were a police dog on the hunt, fearing to speak in case he broke her concentration. He followed her into the sunken living room, where she stopped in front of the entertainment system.

"That's a big TV."

"Maybe he liked movies?" Ethan offered.

"Not movies," Annie corrected. "Video games." She pointed at a set of two video game controllers, which lay exposed on the table. "This place is immaculate, but the controllers are out, just discarded on the table. He must have played often. Maybe with somebody else." She noted a headset that lay next to the main controller.

Annie moved deeper into the apartment, Ethan behind her. They made their way down a hallway, but Annie stopped at a built-in shelf. On its surface sat a candle and a coffee table book on famous architects, but Annie was most interested in the electronic photo frame that ran off batteries. It cycled through a picture every few seconds, and Annie stopped to watch the show.

First, a photo of Tony beneath a *World Video Gamers* banner, a silver medal in his hand. Next, a photo of Tony with his father outside his childhood home, which Annie and Ethan had recently visited. Next, a selfie-style photo of Tony in the coffee shop downstairs, the camera reversed to show him holding an iced latte.

"Not a lotta photos of him with friends, huh?" Ethan asked.

"No," Annie agreed. "And look—" She pulled the frame

off the shelf, holding it in her hands so she could reach the control panel on top. She clicked a button that moved forward through the slideshow, clicking through the pictures at a rapid pace. "Notice anything?"

"They're all recent, except for that one," Ethan said, stopping the slideshow at a picture of Tony graduating college in a cap and gown.

"All the recent pictures have something in common," Annie agreed.

"The necklace," Ethan finally saw it. He pointed to a gold chain around Tony's neck. It led to a charm, dangling outside Tony's shirt. "What is it?"

Annie took a picture of the screen with her phone. Then, she zoomed in, making the small charm larger.

"It's a bird?" Ethan said, noticing the wings by its side.

"A penguin," Annie confirmed. "It's a solid *gold* penguin. Unusual necklace for an adult man."

"Maybe it's his spirit animal," Ethan offered.

"If it is, it's a rather recent innovation," Annie answered, clicking through the photos one more time to compare old to new. "Can we have digital forensics date the images? I want to know when they were taken and work backward to determine when he started wearing the necklace."

"Most definitely," Ethan said, grabbing the frame and tucking it in his bag.

"It's odd," Annie thought aloud. "He's wearing that necklace in every photo, but when he jumped— nothing."

"Body presented no jewelry," Ethan said. "Just his clothes."

Annie didn't respond but allowed the information to percolate as she floated down the hallway toward Tony's bedroom. She entered the grand master suite, which was large enough to fit three king-sized beds. Off to the side, a walk-in closet gleamed, its doors open and inviting. On the other wall sat the entrance to a large master bath. Finally, a set of sliding doors offered entrance to the balcony where Tony fell to his death, their presence ominous and cold.

"Let's divide and conquer," Annie said, her voice naturally dipping to a respectful whisper in the place where her victim had met his end. "Look for anything unusual and flag it for me even if you don't know why you think it's strange. If you spot the necklace, let me know."

Ethan nodded and the pair divided, weaving through the space like metal detectors scouring the sand for spare change. Annie started in the bathroom but found nothing unusual. The claw-foot tub and gleaming marble floor spoke only to immaculate cleanliness. She paused at a toothbrush holder on the sink, locking onto the only thing of note so far: a pair of toothbrushes, each in their own separate compartment. It was possible Tony liked to keep a spare brush, but judging by the fact the bristles on each device were bent, it was clear both toothbrushes were actively in use.

Maybe Tony had a lover, Annie thought to herself. If he did, his father was unaware. Ferdinand would surely have mentioned such an important detail. Still, Annie made a mental note to follow up with him.

"I might have something," Ethan called from inside the walk-in closet. Annie crossed the room to join him, finding him crouched under a hanging space. "It might not mean anything," Ethan said, unsure.

"If you think it's strange, it's worth looking at," Annie prompted.

"I was checking the clothing labels," Ethan motioned across the closet. "This entire side is designer, 'Made in Italy' items. Valentino. Burberry. Kid liked the good stuff. But this hanging space," Ethan motioned to a section lower down. "It's all drop-ship garbage. Not a label in sight."

"I didn't know you were a fashionista," Annie laughed.

"The clothes maketh man. Do you think it means anything?"

"It could just mean he likes to organize his closet by value," Annie pondered. "But these leather jackets," she reached for a line of five brightly colored jackets. "They're just like the one he died in."

"It was faux leather," Ethan added. "What millionaire goes for faux leather when he could afford the real thing?"

"I don't know," Annie agreed, adding the information to her mental filing cabinet. "But we won't forget it. Any sign of the necklace?"

"None," Ethan shrugged. "I opened every drawer. Checked the beside tables. Looked on the floor. Even checked outside on the balcony in case it got caught on something. You?"

"Nothing," Annie said. She strode toward a section of the closet that featured built-in jewelry drawers, opening each one and staring at the contents. Gold bracelets gleamed. Thick chains lay perfectly in place. But the penguin necklace was suspiciously absent. Annie noted that the jewelry looked as if it had been rifled through. A watch was discarded into the wrong compartment. Multiple rings were thrown to the side.

"Tony was organized. He would have kept the necklace here when he wasn't wearing it." Annie pointed at a spot on the top drawer, where a velvet blank space perfectly sized for a necklace lay empty. "It obviously had special meaning to him. It doesn't make sense that it's just— gone." She glanced around the closet, looking at it with fresh eyes. "These shirts are pushed to one side. Was the door open when you came in?"

"It was," Ethan answered.

"Someone was in here. Someone who wasn't Tony."

"We should look for prints," Ethan said. He dug through his pack, pulling out a fingerprint kit. He coated the glass in black dust, stopping when a series of oiled prints emerged. With a steady hand, he pressed tape over the prints, sealing them between glass to take to the lab. "We've gotta a couple. They might be Tony's. Might not be. We'll have to run them through the system."

As if in a trance, Annie moved toward the sliding doors to the balcony, pushing them open and stepping onto the now sacred ground. She looked out at the sea, thinking about Tony and what his final moments must have been like. She crossed her arms on the railing, feeling a warm presence beside her as Ethan did the same.

"What do you think?" Ethan asked.

"I think he was lonely, but not alone. He kept a part of himself hidden, but that's not what got him killed. I think Ferdinand was right, and somebody wanted this apartment."

"Who should we talk to first?"

"The security guard," Annie said, hoping Alfred would be able to provide them with access to security tapes that would shine some light on the events leading up to Tony's death. But from what Annie had already guessed about the nature of secrets at *Rowling Heights,* her next step would likely only lead to questions instead of answers.

CHAPTER FOURTEEN

HATHAWAY

IT WAS late in the evening and Hathaway was feeding his fish, thinking about the meeting that had taken place earlier that day. He hadn't minded seeing Mindy as much as he thought he would. They generally tried to avoid each other when they were doing their business about the building, but of course, the occasional run-in was inevitable. Hathaway sprinkled tiny flakes of crusted protein into the tank— Cataline had left a delivery of essential items by his door earlier that afternoon. He watched as the most colorful fish flapped his tail to reach the surface. Behind him, a dozen more ordinary fish lazily made their way to the top.

Hathaway couldn't help but think that the building reminded him of an aquarium. All of the residents were locked inside, living elbow-to-elbow as they waited for their next meal. He leaned forward, his face casting a reflection across the glass. An almost invisible, little brown fish was ponied up to an orange-and-white specimen, cleaning its tail with his mouth. They were partnered up, the two of them helping each other.

Kind of like marriage, Hathaway thought to himself. He had learned that the tricky thing about marriage was you couldn't help but take on all of your partner's baggage. When Mindy had realized Hathaway came with problems, she didn't want his trouble anymore. And now— even in the midst of a divorce— Hathaway was saddled with the worst of Mindy's decisions.

But all of that was about to change. Hathaway had procured the evidence he needed to invalidate their prenup. The irony was that he couldn't use it until the entire Tony Vasquez case blew over and the right suspect was selected and found guilty. That could take some time.

Hathaway was struck by the urge to go check that his evidence was still in its hiding spot. He had promised himself when he had heard the news of Tony's death that he would leave it untouched in its place until the whole thing had blown over, but now, he was riddled with an itch he needed to scratch. The desire to look at it just one more time swept through him. He needed to know it was real. He spent much of his time alone nowadays. He needed to confirm he didn't imagine the thing, or dream it up on one of his longer, empty nights.

Hathaway stood, crossing into the kitchen, where he kneeled down and felt along the baseboards of the cabinets. The kitchen had yet to be remodeled, as this was a grand but rather old unit. Original, solid wood cabinets hung above a subway tile backsplash. It was the plumber who had come a couple months ago that tipped him off secret drawer. He said he'd seen such a thing before, and that maybe it was used during the Prohibition. Either way, it was a fun feature but never especially useful— until now.

Hathaway felt the wood give beneath his fingers as he pressed down in the proper spot, a popping sound alerting him to the fact the hiding spot had opened. He pulled back the baseboard, revealing a small, secret compartment behind the wood, which had been laid over hidden hinges. The compartment had been built during the Prohibition era, and was just big enough to fit a couple of bottles of wine, or whiskey. But Hathaway had hidden something much more important inside.

He reached his hand into the hole, pulling out a gold necklace. It dangled from his fingers, the chain a decent weight. At the end dangled a single talisman: a solid, gold penguin.

It was unusual jewelry for a man. Hathaway had been pleased with himself when he stole it from Tony Vasquez's apartment. It didn't take much effort to learn Tony's schedule and to sneak up to the eleventh floor when he knew Tony would be away. It had helped that no one else lived on the penthouse floor. He had, of course, worried about the security cameras, but he'd figured out a clever way to mislead anyone who happened to look at the tapes. He was quite sure that Cataline and Alfred never looked at the footage unless there was a complaint. Still, he had made sure to evaluate where the camera on the eleventh floor pointed and had come up with the ruse of pretending to be on a call until he was out of its field of view.

And then— the murderer had happened.

Hathaway held the necklace up to the light, watching the penguin dangle like it was caught in a trap. The necklace proved what he'd been telling the divorce lawyers once and for all. Hathaway was done playing fair. He was willing to do whatever it took to make his ex-wife pay.

CHAPTER FIFTEEN

ALFRED

ALFRED TOOK his time organizing a display case that marked the entryway to *Rowling Heights*. The case was a hallmark architectural feature of the building's original style, and Alfred had dedicated himself to personally ensuring the landmark lobby aspect received a makeover on a monthly basis. Every thirty days, Alfred would adjust the case's contents to reflect a new theme or holiday. It was his personal pet project and he looked forward to receiving compliments from residents and lobby customers with every new design. In December, the case was filled with snow-capped Christmas tree sculptures, elaborate ornaments, and antique dreidels. In late January or early February, it was a testament to Chinese New Year, which varied with the timing of the New Moon. To mark the occasion, Alfred would adorn the case with original red and gold banners and authentic lanterns purchased from a local store in San Diego's Chinatown in the Pacific Historic District. Given that today was the first of May, Alfred was decorating the display case with an elaborate tea party theme to honor the upcoming Mother's Day holiday. A series of boxes sat at his feet, filled with tea cups, teapots, and china plates stacked one on top of the other with bubble wrap keeping their fragile edges separate. He removed a patterned cup from the box, its flower-laced beauty of striking quality.

It was almost enough to distract him from the two detectives hovering over his shoulder.

"No tapes at all from the evening Tony died?" Annie asked. Beside her, Agent Ethan Beckett took notes on a clipboard.

"Unfortunately, no," Alfred said. He positioned the tea cup in the display case, turning it at such an angle as to best reveal its beauty. "The cameras malfunction with terrible frequency. To be candid, we installed them for emotional well-being over function. A boon to our residents' peace of mind."

"Cataline can confirm?"

"Of course," Alfred answered, knowing that Cataline had every motivation to support his account of how the tapes had malfunctioned. She had Mario to consider, and neither one of them wanted him implicated in the murder. Alfred knew his friend well enough that he'd been willing to bet his own future at the building on her love for her son. Their wagons were hitched together, and in many ways, had been for some time.

"A stroke of bad luck, isn't it? That the tapes didn't record on the evening when they were needed most." Annie's face betrayed a comfortable smile. Alfred fixed his eyes on the lid of a teapot he was arranging in the case but caught Annie's reflection in the glass. There was nothing antagonistic in her expression. It was as if she were a curious neighbor rather than a Detective.

"Not if you consider how often they malfunction," Alfred countered. "We have dozens of cameras scattered across the property. At any given moment, at least one of them is likely not recording."

"Sounds like a lot for one person to keep up with," Ethan offered.

"Cataline assists," Alfred said. "But between the two of us, we do the jobs of a dozen people."

"Why do you stay?" Annie asked.

Alfred turned, holding the china plate in his hand with a gentle reverence. "With all due respect, *Rowling Heights* is the finest building on the Western Coast. We stay because we're committed to its legacy, and the residents—" Alfred paused as if he'd thought better of saying what had popped into his mind.

"The residents?"

"The residents are like family," Alfred said. "We work with them every day. We address their needs. We witness their greatest triumphs and biggest defeats. When you support someone in their home environment, it's impossible not to care. Surely you can relate?"

Annie nodded. She often felt a protective sense of guardianship over the victims in her cases, even though they were always people she had never met. It was as if investigating a murderer also brought the victim to life in Annie's eyes, and she became their advocate— their only route to delayed justice in the world they'd left behind.

"I can relate," Annie admitted. She cleared her throat, moving on to a less contentious topic. "We wanted to ask you about the gym and the roof access. They're both on the eleventh floor. "

"That's correct," Alfred confirmed.

"And the only route to either is through the elevators?"

"There are stairs in case of a fire—"

"But even the stairs require a keycard for entry?"

"Yes," Alfred added. "The keycard pads are outside the doors to the stairwell on each floor."

"Wonderful," Annie said. "One final question, before we take too much of your time. The development across the street— the tall building that's under construction. What is it?"

"A new hotel," Alfred waved a hand. "The street gets more crowded every year. When *Rowling Heights* was built it was the tallest building on the row. Now—" Alfred rolled his eyes, communicating his disdain for the structural competition.

"How long ago did they start construction?"

"About twelve months ago," Alfred said.

Annie nodded. This was what she'd been hoping for. "And as to the strange packages— when did you block off access to the roof?"

"Well, about two months ago," Aldred answered, suddenly concerned. "But I can't see what one possibly has to do with the other."

"Maybe nothing, and maybe everything," Annie answered. "Thank you for your time."

With that, she shook Alfred's hand. Ethan offered a simple nod and the two of them disappeared into the hallway that led to the street, leaving Alfred holding a teapot with a paisley print. He turned, placing the teapot on the shelf in front of him. It was one member of a set, complete with plates, china cups, and tiny spoons that provided a unique sense of whimsy. Lined up together, the fragile set looked strong— as if the totality of its parts was sturdier than any individual piece.

Alfred had never lied to law enforcement before. But he was part of a team at *Rowling Heights*. And he would go to any lengths necessary to protect his makeshift family.

CHAPTER SIXTEEN

THE DOOR to the staircase that led to the roof was a wide, metal barrier that stood out from the otherwise pristine decor that trailed the length of the eleventh-floor hallway. Annie and Ethan stood in front of the entryway, staring at a thick chain that had been woven through the handle and secured by a coded padlock.

"They weren't kidding when they said they'd secured the roof access," Ethan said, noticing that the chain was so thick any attempt to saw through it would be unsuccessful. "Sure you don't need to see the gym first?" Ethan nodded down the hallway at a set of sleek glass doors that offered entrance to the building's gym and spa.

"No," Annie answered.

"We have two potential suspects citing the gym as a potential alibi—"

"But the gym doesn't overlook the bay," Annie said, declining to further explain. She bent over the padlock, flicking the numbers on the combination lock into place. "Cataline offered the code without question," she said. "Seemed like she was eager to get me off the phone."

"I can't imagine why," Ethan added, grinning at Annie. "You're the most charming person I know."

With a click, the lock opened. Annie dropped it into her pocket, pulling the chain through the handle until it unwound itself like a snake. It landed on the floor with a heavy thud.

Ethan pulled the door open, revealing a narrow set of stairs. Unlike the rest of the building, no attention had been paid to the aesthetics of the incline. The stairs were metal and barren, and the walls that framed them featured peeling white paint. The lack of exterior windows or overhead lights made it clear this space was never intended for residents. The lack of attention to detail in an otherwise overwrought space made for a creepy effect.

"Age before beauty," Annie nodded at Ethan, who ascended the stairs without question, even though he was only six months older than Annie. Annie followed him, noting a loud humming noise in the background.

"The air conditioning condenser," Annie called out over the hum. Beside her, a rectangular ledge jutted out from the wall, presumably containing the hidden condenser behind the visible access panel. The ledge hung over the stairs at such a low angle that Ethan was forced to duck underneath it to continue his ascent. As he moved, he glanced behind him at Annie, offering her his hand. She took it, and the two of them emerged on the other side.

"Looks like someone was in a rush," Ethan said, pointing at the discarded pieces of cardboard littering the stairwell. Annie bent down to examine the mess, picking up a piece. It looked to be a part of a shipping box's lid, or maybe a side panel, but beyond the fact it was cardboard, the sliver of garbage presented no other useful information. Then, Annie noted something in the corner of the stairwell, beneath the trash. With great care, she removed it from the corner, holding it in the palm of her hand to show to Ethan: a half-smoked cigarette.

"Our cat burglar smokes?"

"Someone does," Annie said, passing the cigarette to Ethan, who quickly pulled a plastic evidence bag from his pack and dropped the cigarette into it without further question. By now, he had learned to trust Annie's hunches. Annie kicked at something near the spot where she'd found the cigarette, then picked it up, showing it to Ethan. It was the tattered remains of a Marlboro Red Label box, the unmistakable brand name still clear.

"Marlboro," Annie said.

Ethan added the box to the evidence bag and continued the ascent. A single flight of stairs later, and the pair stopped at a dead end. Another metal door loomed in front of them, but there was no indication of attempts to lock it or prohibit access except for a simple sign that read: "AUTHORIZED EMPLOYEES ONLY."

Ethan ignored the sign, pushing the door open. Crisp, salty air flooded Annie's senses as she stepped out onto the roof. A full view of the ocean emerged over its edges. The rooftop was littered with the remains of hundreds of ripped cardboard boxes and shipping tape, which had been allowed to spread across the rooftop in a discarded pile. Ethan moved into the center of the space, picking up one box that was still in its original form. He flipped it over, revealing an intact shipping label. "It's just made out to *Rowling Heights*," he said. "No specific unit number or recipient."

"The sender wanted to ensure the packages would sit in the mailroom until he was ready to get them," Annie said. A weather-proof, crumbled coating crackled under her sneakers as she stepped into the sunlight. "He let them pile up, then waited for the right moment to strike. After he moved them, he stored and sorted them here," Annie said, nodding across the rooftop. "It's safe from the elements." She pointed at a storage area cordoned off by two shed-like doors, which were hanging wide open and banging in the breeze.

She strode forward against the wind, stopping at the edge of a waist-high border that marked the edge of the roof. She glanced down at the sidewalk below, thinking about Tony Vasquez's fall. She shuddered, shifting her gaze to the harbor, where the boats were starting to come in for the evening, their sails white drops of paint over an orange blast of a sunset. The light melted against the sea, a harmony of blue and gold creating the kind of balance only found in nature. Then, Annie noticed something strange— red and blue lights on the Northern side of the harbor. Motorboats that had been parked at the DHS building took off in formation, sharks on the hunt, their police lights harsh and out of place against the beauty. The sound of a siren blared in the distance. The boats sped across the turquoise cove, their direction purposeful, a fury of angry waves churning up in their wake.

"The border's there," Annie pointed further down the harbor at a narrow portion of the coastline. "You can see it from here. It's not an actual line but the maps say the legal distinction between the United States and Mexico is right around that ridge."

Annie felt a pair of arms wrap around her waist. It was Ethan, making a rare attempt to hold her. She didn't blame him for trying with such infrequency. He never knew whether she'd accept the gesture or not.

"Right place, right time?" Ethan asked.

"Wrong place. Wrong time. But right person," Annie said, her eyes still fixed on the harbor. She leaned into him. Ethan tracked her gaze, noticing how she followed the boats' movements as if in a trance.

"That's why the DHS put their building where they did. To monitor incoming traffic from boats at sea."

"Nice to know there's people like us out there, trying to make the world a little safer," Ethan said.

Annie didn't answer. She watched the red and blue lights reach across the harbor, their rays illuminating the dark spaces. "I used to think that."

"But the letter?"

"It's someone with access, Ethan. We can't trust anyone. Even people who work for the law, just like us."

Ethan moved his hands down her waist and turned her toward him, away from the lights in the harbor. She wrapped her arms around his neck. "We can trust each other," Ethan said, and Annie nodded. That was something.

"You got a hunch about the DHS?" Ethan asked, bringing the conversation back to the thing he knew Annie was most concerned with.

"This case— it's the same as ours," Annie said. "The people here at *Rowling Heights* put their faith in people and things that were supposed to protect them, but they were wrong."

"You know what happened yet?"

"I have a hunch," Annie smiled. "But suspicions—"

"Aren't facts," Ethan finished Annie's favorite reprise for her. "Then let's find the evidence. Who are we talking to next?"

Annie considered his question, turning around to look once again at the boats, which were now nothing but tiny dots on the horizon. She knew the individual interviews that were to come would change everything, and was determined to have her strategy outlined before she approached the residents she most suspected. Annie balanced on the edge of the building, her palms resting on the ledge, and considered how one wrong move could topple a case, or even a person. Then, she felt Ethan's hands around the belt loops of her jeans, keeping her in place should she slip.

CHAPTER SEVENTEEN

CATALINE

THE BAR CATALINE had chosen as their meeting place was in Old Town, far from the prestige of San Diego's prominent Harbor area. Here, the buildings were worn and built with distinct, individual stones, each of them a testament to the people who had come before. As San Diego's foundational district, Old Town boasted open-air markets selling crafts and handmade souvenirs, winding streets bordered by the iron lampposts of days gone by, and al fresco dining. The historic ambiance of Old Town made Cataline feel as if she'd been transported to another time, the dusty scent of yesterday clinging to the air.

Sitting at a small metal table— a margarita and a basket of chips in front of her— Cataline couldn't help but consider the generations of immigrants who had come to San Diego before her. They'd also had dreams and goals. She wondered if, in pursuing a better life, any of those people from the past had done what she'd done. She wondered if they'd misstepped and been unable to think of a way to course correct.

"It hasn't kicked in yet."

The voice snapped Cataline back into the moment. She

stared at the person across the table— her company for the evening.

Montana smiled back at her. He was *Rowling Heights'* most intimidating resident. At six feet tall and marked by tattoos, Montana also had a sweet side. Even if he *was* a DHS agent and loyal to an organization Cataline loathed.

"The margarita," Montana continued. "It hasn't kicked in yet or you'd be talking more."

"Sorry," Cataline said. "My stomach lately—"

"Understandable," Montana nodded. He pushed food around on his plate as if he were looking to find it a new home. "The investigation has everyone on edge. How far have they gotten?"

"Hard to say. The female detective doesn't miss a thing. But she's quiet about where they're headed."

"You know you have to stay on this. The building is at the center of it all."

"I do."

"It's not just about you anymore, Cataline—"

Cataline laughed. "You think I don't know that? It hasn't been about me for fourteen years. The moment I saw that plus sign, everything changed."

"And I guess I wouldn't know what that feels like?" Montana asked, his cheeks flushing. "So I couldn't possibly relate?"

"That's not what I—"

"It's fine," Montana cut her off, taking a swig of his beer. "I don't want to have the same fight on repeat. Fucking Ground-hog's Day. We are where we are now. I made my choices—" Montana's voice broke a little, but he hid it well. "And you? You made yours. And now we're in this mess together."

Montana's eyes looked over Cataline's shoulder, focused on something in the distance. Cataline turned to locate the source of his interest. Behind her sat a horse and carriage. A brown and white pony whinnied, slamming a hoof into the ground. Behind him, the cart he pulled was stuck in a ditch. The well-meaning rider attempted to push it forward, but the wheel stuck firm in the dirt. Beside him, frustrated passengers watched on, helpless.

"You know, in the bible, they say whoever you're married is more than just a partner. They say you're yoked."

"Yoked?" Cataline asked.

"Like a horse," Montana nodded at the pony. "You're tethered to the other person. Their weight is your weight. You pull their load too, not just your own."

Cataline's eyes watered, but she looked back toward her Margarita, which suddenly held appeal. She took a swig, praying for liquid relief.

"You wanted the meeting," Montana shrugged. "Should probably get to the heart of it."

"I think Mario suspects the truth," Cataline said. "Would that be such a bad thing?"

"You and I had an arrangement."

"Arrangements change."

Cataline slammed her hands on the table. She leaned forward, eyes burning. "Not with me they don't. He's not ready. If I say Mario doesn't need to know, then he doesn't *get* to know. Not until it's safe to tell him."

"Think you made that clear a long time ago," Montana shrugged. "For what it's worth, I didn't say anything."

"You didn't?"

"'Course not," Montana said. "All I do is smile at him in the hallway. Ask him about how school is going. Keep a watchful eye on him." Montana rolled his eyes when he noticed the flicker of doubt that waved across Cataline's face. "Woman, if you don't get it by now, I'm not sure what else I can do for you. Not much left to offer up as proof that you can trust me." He paused, thinking. "Our interests are aligned now more than ever, wouldn't you agree?"

There was a whinnying sound from over Cataline's shoulder. Behind her, the horse surged forward, offering one last, tremendous effort. The cart pulled from the ditch, its wheels finding traction on the road ahead.

Cataline turned back to Montana. "I agree," she said. "That's undeniable now."

"Good," he nodded. "Then instead of focusing on what we can't control or bickering over what's already happened, we got one direction we can move." He nodded at the horse again. It trotted across the road, the attached carriage rolling onward. "Forward. We gotta move forward. There's only one solution to our problem. We need to figure out who had a connection to Tony that would reasonably motivate them to kill him. You know everyone in the building. You must have an idea?"

Cataline mentally flipped through images of each of the potential suspects.

"There might be one," she said. "But I can't do it. It's not right. It's—"

"Our only option. Forward is our only option," Montana said, just as another horse and carriage came around the corner. The truth was, there were hundreds of horses pulling heavy loads, and Montana— he was just one of them. "It's the only way."

"I feel so lost," Cataline said, more to herself than to Montana. "All I've ever wanted was a way out."

"You'll find the way," he nodded at her. "You've always been better at that than I have. Because you follow your heart. *El amor todo la puede*," he said to her, repeating her favorite phrase. Cataline smiled at his broken accent.

"Love conquers all," she agreed, hoping more than ever it was true.

CHAPTER EIGHTEEN

THE BAR and restaurant that rented space on *Rowling Height's* ground floor was a small but upscale enterprise. Annie and Ethan sat in a booth in the corner, situated beneath a chandelier light fixture. Across from them was Mindy Wellington, the finest cut of steak in front of her. She drug the knife in her hand across the taught bit of flesh, cutting on a bias as it split the meat with ease.

"Thank you for allowing us to interrupt your lunch," Annie said to Mindy, who cut into her steak again with a luxurious, slow hand. Mindy was of a class of people who had all the time in the world to enjoy what they consumed. She took a bite, noting the empty spaces on the table in front of Annie and Ethan.

"Of course. You're sure you wouldn't like to join—"

"Oh no," Annie shook her head. "We'll only intrude on your hospitality for a few moments. We'd be finished by the time the appetizers came around."

"You found me because of Alfred, no doubt?"

"An employee of the building may have pointed us in the right direction," Annie hedged. "But I couldn't say which one, specifically."

"That's what I get for keeping a strict routine. This is my treat to myself," Mindy noted, a glimmer in her eye. "The world is hard on women, and every Monday I bring myself to the restaurant and order a steak— rare— and a glass of Cabernet. And I eat in peace and assure myself that the world is mine and there is nothing which might be out of my reach if I only believe I can have it."

"That *sounds* like a treat," Ethan agreed. "Where do I sign up?" Annie elbowed him under the table. "I'd like to start by asking about the view from your apartment window."

"My window?" Mindy said. "What could that possibly have to do with anything?"

"Possibly everything, or also— nothing," Annie said. "I assume, like the other units, your apartment has a view of the harbor?"

"It does," Mindy confirmed.

"And, being on the ninth floor, some of that view has no doubt been obscured by the development across the street."

"Ugh," Mindy clucked her tongue. "We tried to stop that horrible monstrosity from going up in the first place, but the city council approved it despite our efforts. Terrible eye sore. A blight on the community."

"How much of your view is obscured?"

"Not much, fortunately," Mindy answered. "Just the side that looks toward the lighthouse. I prefer the Southern exposure anyway."

"Excellent," Annie smiled as if she'd just received wonderful news. "Onto more important things. How well did you know Tony Vasquez?"

Mindy chewed, but whether that was because the meat was tough or she was buying time was hard to say. Finally, she swallowed. "I knew him as well as any other resident. He came, he went. Our paths did cross more than others, perhaps because I knew him as the man whose father owned the building. And we saw each other at the gym quite often, once I started working out—"

"What made you start exercising?"

"The divorce," Mindy shrugged. "Nobody tells you that the person you marry rubs off on you." Her eyes became distant, memories of what used to be swimming in the dark, brown pools of her irises. "It's a slow process, but if you're not careful, you slowly become more alike. The longer you're married, the more you share certain qualities. The day I woke up and realized I hated Hathaway was a hard one, because we'd been together so long that Hathaway was, well, he was a part of how I defined myself. Once he was gone, I looked for any parts of him that had rubbed off on me. And I saw that he'd made me lazier. Less attractive. I never had time to spend on myself because I was always worried about bettering *him*. Once the problem was brought to my conscious mind, I vowed at once to fix it. So, I started going to the gym every day."

"And Tony was there, too?" Annie asked.

"Yes. Tony liked to use the rower," Mindy shivered at the idea. "I kept my workouts to the Pilates reformer. I've lost twenty pounds," she smiled, taking a sip of her wine. "Imagine that. Eating wine, steak, and chocolate, and *still* I managed to lose twenty pounds without the deadweight of Hathaway sitting on my chest. My girlfriends like to say I lost two-hundred-and- twenty pounds, if you consider his part of the equation—"

"What did you notice about Tony?" Annie attempted to shift Mindy's focus back to the issue at hand. She knew Mindy could turn the entire lunch into a diatribe on Hathaway's faults.

"Notice?" Mindy froze, her fork mid-air. "Nothing."

"Nothing at all?" Annie probed.

"Is that surprising?"

"A little," Annie said. "Most of the other residents were

able to give us at least *some* kind of impression. Surely you noticed something about him, even anything small or insignificant."

Mindy set down her fork and took another long sip of her wine. Annie noticed the way Mindy's upper eyelid twitched as she bought herself time. Mindy was considering the fact that it was more suspicious to notice nothing at all, rather than the most banal elements of a person. She had misstepped. And now, Annie predicted, she would attempt to course-correct.

"Well, of course I noticed *some* things. It's impossible not to notice anything. I may not have thought very hard on it, but I did note a few things about Tony."

"Like what?"

"He rowed like he was going somewhere," Mindy offered. "Tony and I both used our time at the gym with a sense of purpose. Mine was to move past my divorce. His, I think, was to be less lonely."

"Did he tell you he was lonely?"

"No, but it was an impression I had. Just based off a few things he said. He'd mention video game conventions. But it seemed like most of his friends were online. If I had to guess, I'd say he was working out in the hopes of meeting a woman. He seemed—" she paused. "He seemed a little lost. As if he were a ship at sea with no engine, no sails, and no rudder. He was a man who needed a woman. Women fix that. Our presence immediately gives a man a sense of purpose. I assumed that was why he was at the gym. To increase his odds of finding a mate." Mindy returned to her steak, rubbing a piece into the mashed potatoes beside it, then ushering the entire mess into her mouth. "In fact, I thought about setting him up with my friend's daughter," she said, mouth full. "But the girl turned out to be dating someone. A real dumpster of a man according to Victoria. Quite the temper. It's an interesting story, actually. Apparently he popped her car tires because she posted something on social media he didn't like—"

"And Tony," Annie said, again forcing the conversation in the direction she wanted to head. "Was he a good catch, in your opinion?"

For a moment, Mindy didn't say anything. Then, she pushed the potatoes around on her plate. She looked at Annie with narrow eyes, the pace of her speech slowing to a crawl. "Yes," Mindy offered simply. "As I said, I didn't know him very well. But from what *I* could see, he added value to this world. And it's much worse off without him."

Annie nodded, noting the emotion in Mindy's voice. It was all she needed. This single question was the reason she'd hoped to meet with Mindy. And, perhaps, one more.

"Do you know why Tony wore a penguin necklace?"

Mindy was mid-cut when Annie asked the question. Her knife stopped its trail, the inside of the steak bright pink against the metal sheath. A trail of red oozed from the carcass, spilling onto the plate like blood from a wound. Mindy stared Annie dead in the eye, her cadence brittle as bone. "I have absolutely no idea."

"We'll be on our way, then," Annie smiled as if she'd just finished lunch with an old friend. She stood, Ethan in her wake, and the two of them scooted out of the booth, preparing to leave. Annie stopped, turning one last time to speak to Mindy.

"It's missing, you know? The necklace."

Mindy looked up from her steak, and her mouth dropped open. Anger flashed across her face, her cheeks flushing red. Her eyes turned heavy, more bulbous, tears threatening to spill over their edges. And yet, nothing came. Mindy held back the depth of her rage.

Finally, she choked out, "And why should I care about such a thing?"

"You wouldn't," Annie said. "Thank you again, for your time."

With that, they exited, disappearing out the restaurant's slick, curtain-framed doors. When she was sure they had gone, Mindy exhaled, setting down her fork and knife and allowing her head to fall into her hands. She covered her face for a moment, then let the tears that had been threatening to fall all lunch finally streak across her cheeks. She wiped them away, reaching for the wine glass beside her. She gulped down the rest of the glass, thinking about how unfair life could be, and wondering how she'd gotten herself into such a mess. It was her heart, of course. Her heart always misled her, because it beat so loud she couldn't help but listen to it, even when her mind knew the path she was walking was an impossible one.

Mindy glanced out the window again to double-check that the detectives were gone. She scanned the restaurant to ensure no one was watching. Then, she reached under her shirt, pulling out a gold chain.

She held the talisman at the end of the chain in her hand, rubbing it for comfort, clutching it like a protective totem. Her fingers uncurled, revealing the shape underneath:

A solid, gold penguin. His little wings were etched into his side, clumsy feet carved by a skilled artisan who made the small charm seem life-like.

Mindy rubbed it with her thumb, then tucked it back inside her shirt, ensuring it was close to heart.

CHAPTER NINETEEN

ALEJANDRO

ON THE EIGHTH FLOOR, Alejandro was giving his visitors a tour. He showed the detectives a case that lined his living room wall, its glass windows providing a view of *La Vida Liquor* bottles, all of them lined up like little soldiers.

"This, right here," he pointed to a bottle featuring a black label and gold accents. "This is our special edition from last year's crop. The thing about our fermentation process is that it's different than any other brand—"

"Fascinating," Annie agreed. "Back to Tony. Would you say you two were close?"

"No," Alejandro answered. "Not close."

"But we found a dozen liquor bottles in his apartment from your line," Annie added. "Seems like there was a friendship there.

Alejandro inhaled, looking sharply offended. He glanced over Annie's shoulder at Ethan, as if to ask him whether she always behaved in such a feral manner. When Ethan offered nothing in response, Alejandro pulled at the top of his flowing, silk shirt, popping open yet another button. A nest of chest hair revealed itself.

"I'm close to everyone who's anyone on the San Diego social scene. I share my label with my neighbors when they're lucky. My real friends are people worth knowing. I take it neither one of you are drinkers?"

Ethan stepped forward, examining the liquor bottles in the case with a resigned expression. "I drink, but I'm into the cheap stuff. Wouldn't do your brand justice, I'm afraid. Don't have a sophisticated enough palette." He smacked Alejandro on the shoulder, causing him to wobble in place. Alejandro grimaced and stepped away from the case, suddenly agreeing with Ethan. The Detective was right. His product was too sophisticated for these people.

Alejandro slumped onto his snow-white couch, spreading his legs and throwing his arms over the back. "So, you've come to speak to me. What is it you want?"

Annie stood at the floor-to-ceiling windows in Alejandro's unit, looking out at the ocean. "Does it bother you?" She asked, nodding at tall skyscraper that was being built across the street.

"The construction? No. Barely hear it."

"But your view," Annie said. "It's almost entirely obscured. Other units can still see some of the harbor, but yours, I'm afraid—"

"I don't live in the building for the view," Alejandro interrupted her. He noted the blank expressions on Annie and Ethan's faces.

"You don't live here for the view?" Ethan asked, astounded. "Why on Earth would you pay these prices if not for the view."

Alejandro smiled. "For the people. People are the key to everything. *Relaciones.* The key to building businesses. To making money. The value in the building isn't the view. It's the other residents."

Annie strode toward him and sat on the couch, looking him up and down. "That's a nice jacket," she said, motioning to the leather motorcycle jacket that lay over Alejandro's silk shirt. It was a dark blue shade, with silver studs decorating the lapel. "Hand-dyed?"

"Ye- yes," Alejandro stammered. "Imported from Italy."

"I've seen one like it," Annie answered.

For a moment, Alejandro was silent. Then, he looked Annie straight in the eye, curling his fingers around the edge of the couch. "There's plenty of leather jackets in the world."

"Not ones that have been dyed and designed with such precision. You dress well," she said, the edge of an accusation in her voice.

"What are you implying?"

"You know, the last person I saw wearing such a fine leather jacket ended up smashed to bits on the hood of a car."

The air thickened. The room was silent. Ethan shuffled in place, surprised at the turn this had taken. He loved watching Annie untangle a case, but wished she'd let him on her plans every now and then. Instead, he was once again balancing on the edge of a knife, unsure which way the situation might fall.

"So I gave a neighbor fashion advice," Alejandro whispered. "It doesn't mean anything."

"Can we look in your closet?"

For a second, it seemed as if Alejandro might say no. But then, he reconsidered. "If I don't allow you to look, what will happen to me?"

"You and I both know you didn't kill Tony," Annie answered. "But there were other crimes committed, here. Smaller ones, to be sure. But still crimes. I think, perhaps, we could look the other way if you'd help us. Right, Ethan?"

"Sure," Ethan agreed. "I think we could work that out."

"You've told me you value friendship," Annie said, touching the top of Alejandro's hand. "I've accessed the financial records for your liquor business—"

"You had no right! *Cómo te atreves—*"

"The FBI can access any information they deem important to an investigation," Ethan said.

"It seems your business is underwater," Annie continued. "So if you're not surviving off liquor sales, what's really keeping you solvent?" Alejandro didn't answer. "As someone who prizes friendship, maybe you'll understand—you need a friend like me right now."

Alejandro considered what she'd said, then slumped over, allowing the couch cushions to consume his limp floor. "You can look in the closet," he said, defeated. "That way," he pointed toward a hall that led to the bedroom.

Annie stood, walking down the hallway, Ethan in her wake.

"I didn't kill him," Alejandro called out from the living room, adding the important detail just as Annie entered the bedroom. It was similar to the layout of Tony's master suite but smaller, and less impressive. Annie strode toward the walk-in closet and flicked on a light. There, dozens of similar leather jackets lined the hanging space. On the floor sat familiar cardboard boxes, opened and discarded.

"He found out," Alejandro added. Annie and Ethan jumped at the voice behind them. Alejandro stood in the doorway, shadows falling over his face. "We hit the gym together some days. That's why my card was buzzed to the eleventh floor. We'd work out. He invested in my liquor business, but he didn't know I was moving money around between the clothes and the booze. And when he realized what I was doing, I begged him not to tell his father—"

"The labels are removed, then?"

"Sometimes we sew designer labels back in. Sell them as the real thing," Alejandro conceded. "It's the only thing keeping me going. The margins on the liquor label are thin. I moved cash out of the clothing game to support the bottles. I told Tony if he went to his Dad, he'd ruin the entire enterprise and I'd go under, which would have been bad for both of us.

Seeing as he invested in the liquor, we were tied together. The catch is, the guy is rich. He would've recovered. But me? Not so much. He understood my situation. He kept it to himself, just to be kind."

"So you gave him a jacket?"

"As a thank you," Alejandro said. "When I gave him the *maltido* jacket, I never thought he'd wear it all the time. Not sure why he did."

"Because he really did consider you a friend," Annie said. "Not the way you use the word, but the way it was meant to be used. It reminded him of a time he helped someone he thought he could trust."

"*La mierda*. When you say it like this— I feel awful—"

"But you didn't need a view?" Annie asked, suddenly disappointed. "You never needed the view."

"What view?" Alejandro asked, clearly lost.

"Why did you use the roof to store the packages?" Annie clarified, suddenly bothered. She'd walked the wrong trail, and it had only led her to new questions.

Alejandro motioned around the room. "I told you, I have a lot of friends. If someone found out, they could turn me in. It seemed safer, storing shipments on the roof until Alfred got involved."

"Thank you," Annie said. "That's all we need for now."

With that, she turned on her heel and Ethan followed. They left Alejandro at the entrance to his closet, surrounded by merchandise, the truth of who he was sitting heavy on his shoulders. He blinked, a little surprised at himself, then ran after them, stopping them at the front door.

"Hey," he said. "If it helps at all, somebody else was also using the roof. Not to store anything, but there were time I found burned cigarettes up there. It's a non-smoking building, so I figured someone was just looking for a place to light one up. But maybe—"

"Maybe," Annie agreed, also considering the possibility.

"I hope you find the person that did this to Tony," Alejandro added. "He really was what you said. *Un verdadero amigo.* A true friend."

CHAPTER TWENTY

MONTANA

MONTANA'S APARTMENT was the least impressive specimen they'd seen so far. His decorating skills— or lack thereof— were partly to blame. His furniture looked second-hand, as if he had collected it all from street corners and garage sales. A brown couch with fraying threads divided the living room in half, its worn fabric begging to be reupholstered. A beat-up lazy boy was tucked into the corner, its leg resting in the unfolded position, rips in the forest-green leather hastily remedied with duct tape. A forlorn rug completed the scene, the dust coating its edges bearing witness to the fact that it hadn't been vacuumed since Montana purchased it a year ago.

"Nice place," Ethan nodded, oblivious to the look Annie shot him out of the corner of her eye.

"It's alright," Montana held up a hand, settling into the lazy boy, his body sinking into an indentation that perfectly fit his form. "You don't have to lie. We both know it's a shithole."

Compared to the other units in the building, Montana's apartment did lack a certain glamour. Annie's eyes scanned the room, noting that the space was half the size of the others they'd seen, devoid of any luxurious touches, such as marble floors or custom cabinets. The kitchen was a standard galley. The floors were cheap vinyl. And, worst of all, the living room lacked the floor-to-ceiling windows and decadent view of the harbor they'd seen in other apartments at *Rowling Heights.*

She stood, crossing to the only flat, square window in the space. It was covered by horizontal slatted blinds, which Annie pulled open. The view was simple. To the left, a small glimpse of blue water resting in the harbor. To the right sprawled skyscrapers and the construction project Annie had noticed days ago.

"Not much to write home about," Montana said, watching as Annie took in the view.

"No," Annie agreed. "It's a shame. Being on a lower floor seems to have deprived you of the best the building has to offer."

"Nah," Montana shook his head. "I got what I came here for."

"And what's that?" Annie asked.

"A fresh start," Montana said. The tone in his voice indicated he preferred not to elaborate on the exact nature of the fresh start he sought.

"You work for the Department of Homeland Security?"

"That's right," Montana agreed. "I oversee a group of agents responsible for customs. You know those border checks you gotta go through?"

Annie and Ethan nodded.

"Well, the pain in your ass is me," Montana said. "You wouldn't believe the things that come through. We keep Americans safe, mostly."

"Mostly?"

Montana lowered the footrest on his Laz-E-Boy, leaning forward, arms crossed. "It's a big job. Can't do it perfect all the time. There are days we miss things. Gets to you. I'm sure you understand."

"Yes," Annie agreed. "We do." Annie sat down on the couch, touching as little of it as possible, her rear end occupying only the slightest edge. Ethan bit his lip to keep from laughing, noticing how Annie crossed her hands in her lap so as not to touch the dust-infected fabric. "How well did you know Tony?"

"Not at all," Montana said. "Saw him at the gym sometimes but never talked."

"And you were at the gym the day of Tony's murder?"

"It was leg day," Montana said without a care. "I would've been there, but don't remember anything special happening. If the keycard says I was on the eleventh floor, well, that's the only reason why I ever head upstairs."

"Is there anyone who can validate you were there that day?"

"Maybe not that day," Montana added. "But Mario— Cataline's son— he can back the fact that I'm in the gym a lot."

"Mario?" Annie said, surprised.

"Yeah," Montana answered. "The kid and I work out together sometimes. He's a shrimp. I'm helping him bulk up."

"And Cataline's alright with that?"

"'Course she is. Only one who seems to have a problem with it is you," Montana rolled his eyes.

Annie took this in, her mind attempting to sort what was relevant to the case from what was simply noise. She ran through her mental checklist of Montana's backstory. He was a DHS agent. His personality profile described a person who was tough on the outside, but soft within. He was a creature who didn't like change, appearing to keep jobs and homes for as long as possible. He had stayed at his last apartment for a decade before moving to *Rowling Heights*, which presented an exorbitant financial shift upwards.

"The tenant records stated you moved in eleven months ago."

"Sounds right."

"Why *Rowling Heights?*"

"Why not *Rowling Heights?*" Montana countered.

"You don't have a view," Annie motioned at the window. "You're paying a premium to live in this building when it offers you so little. And you don't strike me as the type who cares about prestige."

"It's close to the office," Montana offered. "The DHS building is right around the other side of the Harbor. Take the frontage road straight down and you'll get there. Two-minute drive at most."

"Yes," Annie smiled. "The DHS building. I'm familiar with it. Did you know that other apartments in this building have a view of the DHS building?"

"I had no idea," Montana shrugged, but the way his eyebrows raised made Annie believe he did know, and was choosing to feign ignorance.

"Not all the apartments, though," Annie continued. "Only one, in fact."

Montana didn't answer. Annie let the silence sit, then chose to move on. "This building was quite a financial step up for you. You're paying almost double what you did at the last place."

"So?" Montana asked.

"How can you afford it?"

"Well," Montana said with a tone that made it clear he thought this should all be obvious to anyone with half a brain. "I can afford it because I did such a great job saving money at the last place." He glanced at Ethan. "Is she for real?"

"Watch it," Ethan said. Annie touched his knee, signaling she was unphased.

"What's your impression overall of the residents in this building?" Annie asked brightly.

"Stuck up rich people who ended up renting," Montana said. "If I had their money I'd be smart enough to buy a place, but hey, what do I know? I had just enough to make this work but not enough for a down payment. Got to the point in life I started valuing experience and I took the plunge. Those people though—"

"You think they value the wrong things in life?"

"Guess so, but what do I care as long as I get mine," Montana said.

"And what about the people who work here? Alfred... Cataline."

Annie noticed that Montana's hand flinched when she said Cataline's name. He reacted as if she'd stung him.

"They're fine," Montana said. "They seem to go out of their way to make these people happy."

"In your opinion, do you believe can we trust Cataline and what she tells us?"

There was a long pause as Montana leaned in. "Lady," he said, shaking his head. "If being in the line of work I'm in has taught me anything, it's that I don't think you can trust nobody. Not me. Not Cataline. Not the DHS. Not Alfred. Not the stuck-up richies that live here." He leaned back in his chair. "But you already knew that. So what the hell are you asking me for?"

Annie smiled. "Your apartment," she said. "There's a distinct smell—"

"I don't clean well. What of it?" Montana bristled.

"No, it isn't that. Ethan, do you smell it?"

Ethan nodded in agreement. "I do."

"Care to tell our new friend what it is?"

"Cigarette smoke," Ethan said.

"Did you know the building was non-smoking?" Annie asked.

"Course I know. Just don't give a fuck," Montana answered. "What's it to you?"

Annie thought of the small, burned cigarette butt she'd found on the roof, which was currently sitting inside an evidence bag in Ethan's backpack. She wondered if she should reveal her hand now but thought better of it. There were still so many questions to answer.

"What brand do you smoke?" Annie asked.

"Camels, only."

Annie noted the information, her disappointment flashed across her face. "Can we see them?"

Exhausted and thoroughly frustrated, Montana shifted, reaching into his pocket and extracting a package of Camels. Using an underhand toss, he threw them to Annie, who caught them in both hands. She opened the box to be sure. The cigarettes inside were camels, just as he'd claimed.

"Anything else you need?" Montana hedged. "Prostate exam? Childhood traumas?"

"No," Annie said. "This will do," she paused. "At least, for now."

———

Later, Annie and Ethan strolled down the hallway outside Montana's apartment, making their way to the elevator while considering the facts of the case.

"You think he's clean?" Ethan asked.

"About as clean as you and I are, meaning, completely dirty. But the cigarettes—"

"They don't match," Ethan finished Annie's sentence for her. "The one we found on the roof was a Marlboro. He smokes Camels."

"Maybe he doesn't smoke them all the time?"

"Could be. You think he's intentionally misleading us?" Ethan asked.

"He didn't strike me that way," Annie said. "He's nothing if not direct. And he didn't know we were coming today. He already had them on hand."

A ringing sound emanated from Ethan's pocket. He pulled out a black FBI-issued burner phone.

"Yes?" He waited, listening to the voice on the other end. "Really? And you're sure? Degree of certainty?" Again, the voice on the line muttered. "Got it. Thank you."

Ethan hung up the phone, sliding it back into his pocket just as the elevator arrived.

"We've got an I.D. on the fingerprints from Tony's closet," he said, just as Annie was reaching for the lobby button. "You might want to send us to the tenth floor."

"Hathaway?" she smiled, happy to finally see one of her suspicions proven correct during this investigation. "Excellent."

Annie hit the button for the tenth floor, the elevator doors closing gently behind them.

CHAPTER TWENTY-ONE

HATHAWAY

HATHAWAY'S TENTH-FLOOR apartment had suffered greatly from the fallout of the divorce proceedings. It was a shadow of its old self—collateral damage in the war between its parents. The custom kitchen cabinets lacked a certain sheen, affected by a lack of polishing. Mindy used to remind the maid service to attend to them with wood cleaner, but now, they were left to suffer under direct exposure to the sunlight pouring in through the massive windows across the living room. The place was hardly tidy, with Hathaway's paperwork spread across every table and every chair. Mindy would never have allowed such chaos.

"Got it as soon as she left," Hathaway directed Annie and Ethan's attention to the one-hundred-gallon fish tank that sat on the credenza in the living room. "Mindy didn't want us to have pets. Said she knew I wouldn't walk a dog or feed a cat. But she never stopped to think of fish."

He watched the tropical beasts swimming around the tank. Their fins waved past the glass in multi-colored swirls, strange edges giving the impression of a beast from another era, Prehistoric or Jurassic.

"Your view is lovely," Annie said, taking in the scene out

the window. She was standing by the far wall of the living room, while Ethan was seated on the couch. Before her, the harbor glittered, the sun turning the water gold. "Shame about the construction," she added, noting the skyscraper in the distance. "Blocks half your view."

"Yes, it's been a nuisance. Why did you want to talk to me again?" Hathaway asked.

Annie joined Ethan on the couch, suddenly serious. "We've come across a bit of a mystery no one seems to be able to solve," Annie answered.

"A bigger mystery than who killed Tony?"

Annie pushed a photograph across the coffee table. Hathaway leaned in to examine it: there was Tony, his arms spread wide in triumph at the top of a mountain hike.

"This was on his Instagram page," Annie said. "It was taken a couple of months before he was killed. Notice what he's wearing?"

"The red leather jacket?" Hathaway answered. "He wore that thing everywhere. Stupid, to wear it hiking."

"Not the jacket. The necklace."

Hathaway blanched at the mention of the necklace but leaned in anyway, appearing to examine the photo more closely. "The gold one? Haven't seen it," Hathaway said, suspiciously answering a question that Annie hadn't asked.

"Do you know why he wore it? It seemed to mean something to him. It's in every photo going back about some months."

"He never said," Hathaway shrugged. "Never occurred to me to ask. Didn't know him that well."

"I see," Annie said.

"I've been rather wrapped up in my own mess," Hathaway added, motioning at the stacks of paperwork that filled the room. "Never thought the most complicated case I'd tackle would be my own divorce. We had a strong prenup in place, which necessitates certain payouts with the exclusion of certain clauses. If 'x' then 'y' kind of thing. It's all about trying to find the loopholes."

"How is it coming along?"

"Nasty," Hathaway said. " But that's to be expected, when two people tied themselves together forever without even knowing how long 'forever' could feel." Hathaway paused, straightening his tie. "You have to be careful who you attach yourself to. I've learned that now."

"Is there someone you're attached to now that Mindy's out of the picture?"

Hathaway nodded at the tropical fish tank. "Just them, for now."

"Thank you," Annie stood. "We apologize for wasting your time. There's just no way to be sure someone doesn't have helpful information if we don't ask—"

"Not a problem at all," Hathaway smiled. "I hope you find out about the necklace. Especially if it's related to, you know —" Hathaway drug a finger across his neck in a slicing motion. "And you do think it is, uh, related?"

"Oh most definitely," Annie nodded. "And we will find out what it means. Tony's father reported that he received a call from Tony the day he was killed. Tony told him someone had broken into his place. Rummaged through his closet. Stolen the necklace."

"Oh my," Hathaway said, cheeks flushing. "That does sound incriminating."

"We've filed the warrant to search the place. We're waiting on the approval to come tomorrow morning. We'll take fingerprints," Annie lied, her voice casual. She didn't care to let Hathaway know they'd already run the prints and found a match for his own fingers. "Should be enlightening."

"I wish you luck with that," Hathaway said, thankful the pair was making their way to the front door. "You let me know if there's anything else I can do."

He shut the door behind them, slumping against it, chest

heaving. Panic sparked beneath his skin, an electric shock repeating the same message over and over.

They know. They know. They know.

But they didn't know. At least, not yet. And if they suspected what he'd done, they certainly couldn't prove it. It struck Hathaway that he should have worn gloves when he searched Tony's place. But of course, the decision to break in had been on impulse. He'd been angry about another one of Mindy's demands. He knew better. He was smarter than this. Or perhaps Mindy was right and he was good for nothing.

Hathaway sank to the floor. He needed to make this right. And there was only one way to reverse the damage he'd done.

CHAPTER TWENTY-TWO

CATALINE

IN CATALINE'S EYES, today was a day where nothing could go right. She'd woken up with a headache after a sleepless night spent tossing and turning beneath a comforter she'd let go too long without washing. She tried to blame her restlessness on the dishes that had piled in the sink, or concerns about Mario's sudden struggle in math class, but she knew her inability to get some shut-eye was due to something else:

The Detectives.

They'd been interviewing everyone in the building. They'd cornered Mindy at her usual Monday brunch, and Alfred had reported that they'd caught Hathaway in the evening. Montana had personally let Cataline know he'd been interviewed, as had Alejandro, in a colorful text message that used words Cataline couldn't repeat in front of her son.

Now, she was trying to get Mario out the door for school, but every question was met with a problem.

"Did you get a sweater?" Cataline asked Mario, shoving a peanut butter and jelly sandwich into a bag.

"It's not cold enough," he said.

"What about your math homework?"

"It's on my desk."

"Don't you think it needs to be in your backpack, *mijo*? Or are we expecting your teacher to swing by for dinner later tonight?"

Mario mumbled something she couldn't hear, then took off to his bedroom to get his homework. He hadn't forgiven her for taking the package he'd removed from Tony's front door away from him. He'd asked a question about it every day since. Once Mario was stuck on an idea, he wouldn't let it go.

Cataline finished packing Mario's lunch just as he emerged with his math homework, which he stuffed into a folder.

"Can I go now?" He asked, looking like Cataline had told him he couldn't get a puppy.

His distress stirred something within her. Cataline put her hands on his shoulders, pulling him close. "Miho," she said, "I'm sorry you can't have the package. But you have to believe me that it will only lead to trouble. Trust that there is a reason for this. It's because I love you. *El amor todo lo puede,*" she repeated the phrase she'd been drilling into Mario since his birth. *Love conquers all.*

She felt Mario nod, but he didn't say anything else. He grabbed his bag and headed to catch the bus, barely looking over his shoulder.

" *Te amo mucho,*" Cataline called after him. There was no response. The door shut behind her son, and for the first time all morning, Cataline was alone. She leaned against the kitchen counter, craving a vice. She tried to resist, but on a day like to today, it was necessary.

Stepping on a small two-step ladder, Cataline reached upwards to open the cabinet where she kept things Mario wasn't supposed to have— the one that was too high for him to reach. First, she removed the package that Mario had refused to stop asking about. The shipping label was addressed to Tony Vasquez, with the penthouse's unit number printed on the front. She opened the brown box, pulling out what was inside.

It was a small, rectangular kit barely bigger than her hand, wrapped in laminate plastic. The brightly colored label on the kit read "GENEOLOGY TO YOU." A subtitle underneath advertised: "Find your heritage. 100% secure."

A DNA test. Cataline shivered at the thought. It frightened her that Mario was old enough to introduce this kind of chaos into their lives using subterfuge. She shuddered at the idea the day might come when she might not fully know her son.

It was a thought so disturbing that Cataline didn't even feel the usual guilt that came with indulging her greatest vice. She reached back into the cabinet and pulled out a lighter and a pack of cigarettes.

It was a bad habit she'd picked up many years ago, and one she was careful never to allow her son to see her indulging. Cataline only smoked far away from Mario, and only when she'd had a particularly stressful day— something that had become increasingly common over the past six months.

Cataline clicked the lighter, letting the end of a single cigarette burn orange. She brought it to her lips, savoring the familiar scent, inhaling then exhaling with nerve-tingling relief. She set the package down on the counter, the label face-up.

The red and white packaging was iconic and impossible to miss: Marlboro Red Label.

Cataline took another puff, letting her vice bring her comfort in a difficult moment. To Cataline, the cigarettes felt like a reprieve— little did she know, they might become her downfall. Cataline enjoyed every inhale, blissfully unaware that right now— in an evidence bag in Agent Ethan Beckett's backpack— a similar Marlboro cigarette sat in suspension, waiting for its owner to be discovered.

CHAPTER TWENTY-THREE

HATHAWAY

HATHAWAY WASN'T sure how he'd arrived at this moment in life. He was aware, of course, of the technical steps he had taken to arrive outside Tony Vasquez's door. He had waited until the cleaning crew passed by his floor and stolen a key card off the cart of an unassuming maid. He wasn't about to make the same mistake twice and use his own card to scan himself to the penthouse level. When night had fallen, Hathaway had buzzed himself up the elevator, checking that the hallway was empty before walking to Tony's apartment.

Hathaway was clear on the literal movements that had brought him to this moment—but the emotional decisions behind the steps bewildered him. Why had he allowed his ex-wife to affect him this way? Was the divorce driving him crazy? Maybe he was alone too much, his only company the fish in his aquarium. He should have gotten a dog as a companion, but Mindy had made him feel he was incapable of caring for any living creature. He'd let his ex-wife's impression of him affect his self-esteem, and his perception of his personhood had warped so much that "criminal" didn't seem like a bad label to apply.

Now, he stood in front of Tony's door for the second time in a matter of days. He'd planned to break into the lock the same way he had on the evening Tony was killed: with brute force, and a skinny metal device he had ordered off the internet after watching a YouTube tutorial on how to pick locks. This time, however, no pick was needed. The door opened with ease. It looked as if nobody had bothered to repair the lock since Hathaway had broken it in the first place. They'd all been too busy trying to solve Tony's murder.

Hathaway stepped into the foyer, a black duffel bag in hand. The smell in the apartment made his nose burn. It smelled like old gym clothes and microwave TV dinners. Tony didn't get out much. But then again, neither did Hathaway.

Hathaway took a deep breath, trying to remember what steps he had taken the night he'd stolen the penguin necklace from Tony's apartment. Not wearing gloves during that first break-in was a stupid move. As a lawyer, Hathaway should've known better than to leave behind incriminating evidence like fingerprints. He'd never expected Tony to end up *murdered* just a few hours later. Hathaway thought he was engaging in a minor, emotional misdemeanor. Not lining himself up to be a suspect in a murder.

Hathaway dropped his duffel bag and removed a bottle of Windex spray, along with a rough towel. He pulled out a pair of latex gloves, snapping them on each hand with a determination that said he'd learned from his mistakes. He'd made a terrible lawyer throughout his career but was determined to be a better criminal. He started at the front door, wiping down the handle. Then, he moved through the living room. He'd opened multiple drawers while looking for the necklace but thankfully hadn't spent much time in the main living space. It had occurred to him early on that Tony would keep jewelry beside his clothes.

Satisfied with his work, Hathaway made his way to the

master bedroom, stopping when he reached the walk-in closet. He wiped down the handle. The mirror. And finally, the built-in jewelry drawers, where he'd ultimately found the small, gold trinket in the shape of the world's clumsiest bird.

He'd never understood why the two of them had chosen a penguin to represent their connection. Any true romantic would pick something graceful, like a swan, or an egret. Penguins were impractical birds incapable of doing the one thing birds were meant to do— fly.

Hathaway loomed over the drawer where he'd ultimately found the necklace. It was still empty, an indentation in the cushion indicating the something valuable had once lain on the soft, cloth pillow. Hathaway remembered how he'd felt when he'd stolen the necklace that night. First, he had removed his cell phone and taken a picture of its resting place in Tony's closet, surrounded by clothes that undeniably belonged to the man. That was all he had planned to do— take a photo as evidence and leave. But when presented with the token that night, Hathaway had felt an unexpected rage rise within him. The penguin did not belong to Tony. Not really. The penguin should have been *his*, as stupid a creature as it was. The whiskey he'd had earlier that day had bubbled up in his throat. Hathaway remembered how he'd felt in that moment. He'd felt like he wanted to deprive Tony of something. Hathaway had wanted revenge.

And that was why he'd taken the necklace. Hathaway had wanted Tony to know how it felt to lose something treasured. Something valuable.

It was the whiskey that had made him do it. And now, he was a suspect in a murder investigation. But not if they couldn't find his fingerprints.

Hathaway sprayed the case again for extra measure, then wiped it clean. His reflection appeared in the mirror behind the armoire, a hazy facsimile of the man he used to be.

Hathaway thought of the fish in his aquarium and

wondered if they too often caught their own reflections in the tank. Did they hate to look at themselves as much as he did?

Life, Hathaway thought, was determined by who you tied yourself to. By the allegiances a person chose. Hathaway had tied himself to Mindy long ago, and the recent effort of attempting to untangle what they'd built had changed him. And yet, some piece of him would always feel a connection with her, even as they were trying to destroy each other.

Hathaway slipped out of the closet, shutting the door behind him with a final, silent click.

CHAPTER TWENTY-FOUR

CATALINE.

CATALINE WAITED for Alfred at a small table in the corner of the coffee shop that sat in *Rowling Height's* lobby. This was their tradition, and Cataline thought fondly of the hours they'd spent brainstorming ways to make the residents' lives better. Before the rest of the world was even awake, Alfred and Cataline were already at work, determined to improve the building they'd tied themselves to. Cataline and Alfred had formed a friendship over their mutual loyalty to *Rowling Heights.* But there was one person who came even before the building for Cataline. One person in the world who had her loyalty over all others:

Mario.

Cataline reminded herself that she was doing this for him.

Just then, Alfred took his seat. He smiled at her as she pushed a croissant across the table at him.

"The usual," she said.

"I'd expect nothing less," Alfred answered. "What's on the itinerary today?" He opened up the pastry, taking a generous bit before washing it down with a cup of coffee Cataline had already ordered for him.

"Well, the cleaning ladies are upset again. They say it's too hard to keep up with the hallways and the residents simply throw their garbage outside their doors, waiting for it to be hauled away—"

"A fair complaint."

"And then there's the problem with the HVAC. The entire unit needs replacing but the last word from Ferdinand was we should try to delay as long as possible—"

"I doubt that's changed now, given what he's going through," Alfred said, a heavy sadness in his voice.

"Yes," Cataline said, adjusting the collar on her shirt. "Speaking of that... I had an idea. A way we might offer a pick-me-up to the residents in the midst of all the sadness."

"Anything," Alfred nodded.

"Well, the display case in the lobby? I thought maybe we could change it to a resident appreciation display."

"But I've just set it up for Mother's Day," Alfred answered, surprised. It wasn't like Cataline to dictate the decoration in the display case. She knew this was his pet project— the thing he was most proud of and his own personal touch on the building.

"And it's *beautiful*," Cataline said quickly. "The teapots are wonderful. Everyone stops to look. I don't know where you sourced them but they're lovely. It's just— I wonder if the building needs a feeling of unity right now."

"Do you think so?" Alfred asked.

"Yes. The investigation has been so disruptive. It's divisive. Everyone thinks that one of our own killed Tony. It makes the air heavy. There's this feeling of mistrust in the air. Have you noticed it?"

Alfred couldn't disagree. Since Tony's death, there *had* been a different energy in the building. People spoke to each other less in the hallways. Residents came to him with fewer complaints. It was the same type of stillness that came before a storm when all the animals chose to hide inside their dens. It seemed as if the residents of the building were lying low. "I have noticed it's been quiet," Alfred said.

"Because they've lost trust," Cataline agreed. "They believe someone in this building murdered Tony. I've had three requests this week alone to terminate leases early—"

"No!" Alfred exclaimed.

"Yes," Cataline said, shaking her head. "And I've had exactly zero inquiries about vacant units. Thankfully we're at full capacity, but I don't have to tell you what the numbers mean. Tony's death has been all over the press. In every newspaper. If we're not careful, *Rowling Heights* could become known as the building where something bad happened. *Una casa de Muerte.*"

"But you and I both know it's so much more than that," Alfred said, thinking of the hours he'd spent making sure the building lived up to its full potential.

"Of course, but that's not the worst of it. If the current residents move out when their leases end, and no one knew moves in, well... I don't have to tell you what could happen."

Alfred pictured his beloved building empty, devoid of friendly figures in the hallways, the immaculate first-floor shops and restaurants a ghost town without residents to populate the space.

"I think we need to feature the residents who are suspects in the investigation in the display case to assuage the feeling of fear. We need to remind people that we're a family here. And I don't care what those detectives say. No one in *Rowling Heights* would've killed Tony."

Alfred nodded. He didn't think anyone in the building had the capacity for murder, either.

"Can you do this for me?" Cataline asked. She slid an envelope across the table. Alfred opened it. Inside were photographs of each resident that had been named in the investigation. Mindy. Hathaway. Alejandro. Montana. And of course, a picture of Cataline, and one of Alfred himself. "You could put a bio next to each picture in the display that humanizes the person. Something that reminds everyone we're all in this together."

Alfred thought wistfully of his teapots. He'd worked hard on that display. But as Cataline had pointed out, there was a greater cause to which he was bound. The future of *Rowling Heights* was more important than his pride in his teapot display.

"Consider it done," Alfred assured her.

———

Later, Cataline closed the door to her apartment, thankful that Mario was at school and that the needs of the building had been attended to, affording her a thirty-minute break that was hers and her alone. She slumped down on the couch, taking a deep breath in and letting the subsequent exhale leak from her lungs like air from a tire. She felt a sharp pang of guilt at manipulating her old friend into doing something he otherwise would have never considered. But she needed to protect her family. She needed to assure Mario's future.

She stared at the ceiling for a while, arms spread wide over the couch's pillows. Then, she reached into her pocket, pulling out her cell phone.

CHAPTER TWENTY-FIVE
MONTANA

MONTANA DIDN'T ENJOY DOING bad things. But somehow, bad things seemed to find him and declare that they needed doing. It was as if he were born with a connection to a cosmic to-do list that featured only the worst possible acts, and he was the sole person destined to carry them out. Life had come at him that way— one nasty necessity at a time. And Montana was the kind of man who did what needed to be done.

He thought about that fact as he stood in front of the door to Hathaway's tenth-floor apartment, tapping the lock with a hammer hovered over the metal end of a screwdriver that he placed in the keyhole. A few solid hits and— bang— the lock broke apart. He turned the knob and the door swung open, granting him access to Hathaway's home.

Hathaway's apartment wasn't anything to write home about. In fact, Montana thought, it looked much like his own. Devoid of any decoration or pleasant effect. It was a home built on utilitarian design and was worse off for it. Except for the fish. The fish were a nice touch.

Montana bent down in front of the aquarium, watching the tropical fish swim in circles behind the glass. They carved hypnotic trails through the freshwater, their tails a shimmering web of spots and stripes.

As smooth as those fish, Montana moved on, weaving his way through Hathaway's apartment. He opened every drawer in the living room, seeking something in particular. He flipped on the bedroom light, checking under the pillows and on the nightstand. He was careful to put everything back in the exact place he'd found it, leaving no stone unturned while also avoiding hints as to his presence. Montana could be a ghost when needed. This wasn't his first rodeo.

He moved back into the kitchen, considering what he knew about the building. It had been constructed during prohibition— Cataline had told him as much. She'd also said the units were originally identical but had been upgraded over time to look different from each other. Montana noticed that Hathaway's apartment bore a resemblance to his own. Both apartments had the same layout. The same windows. The same kitchen cabinets. Hathaway's place had a better view, for which he certainly paid a premium price, but otherwise, their units were similar.

Montana walked toward the kitchen, feeling under the baseboards. He'd discovered the quirk in his own kitchen cabinets weeks after move-in. It was a fun, hidden surprise that spoke to the building's history.

Montana's fingers felt a cut-out in the baseboard paneling. He pushed, and the secret compartment clicked open, just as it did at his own apartment. Montana felt inside, scarcely able to believe anyone would choose to hide something in such a compartment. It was foolish, to act like a child, keeping items in secret drawers. Real men knew things of importance were best hidden in plain sight. But then again, from what Montana knew of Hathaway, he wasn't the brightest bulb in the box.

Sure enough, Montana felt something at the back of the

compartment. He pulled it out, revealing a chain with a gold figurine attached— a pendant in the shape of a penguin.

Montana smiled, tucking the necklace into his pocket. He took one long, sad glance around the place, thinking about the things he had in common with Hathaway. They were both single. Both jilted. And both criminals. It was a shame Hathaway had to go down like this, but Montana knew what had to be done.

To protect the people he loved— to protect the people he'd tied himself to— Montana had to commit an unfair act against Hathaway. This had to done because Montana would always prioritize the people he loved most.

Montana might be a criminal, but he was a criminal who knew where his loyalties lay.

CHAPTER TWENTY-SIX

THE MOTEL ROOM they'd booked was a shamble of a thing located in San Diego's old town. Annie rolled over in bed, taking in her surroundings as she so often did late at night when the rest of the world was asleep. Floral wallpaper covered every wall. Heavy drapes obscured the window, which— when uncovered— offered a disappointing view of the flat, asphalt parking lot.

Annie stared at the cottage-cheese ceiling, thinking about the facts of the case so far.

"What is it?" Ethan's voice cut through the silence. They'd booked two motel rooms so as not to tip off the FBI as to the personal nature of their relationship. But from the start of the trip, they'd only used one room. Annie was giving the idea of closeness a chance. But still, sometimes she would forget there was someone sleeping next to her, and Ethan's presence would surprise her.

"Nothing," Annie said.

Ethan rolled over, moving closer to her, resting his head on his hand. "It's never nothing."

"I keep thinking about what Ferdinand said to us."

"Remind me."

"He said the key to understanding the people in the building was figuring out who they'd tied themselves to. Where their loyalties lie."

"You think that has something to do with the case?"

"Yes," Annie said.

"How close are you to breaking it wide open?"

"Nearly there."

"But there's more?" Ehtan asked.

Annie didn't answer.

"Not about the case," Ethan said. "There's more bothering you, and it's not about who killed Tony. It's something else."

Annie stared into his eyes, moved by how well Ethan could read her. It made her feel both understood and afraid at the same time. In the presence of the rest of the world, Annie could hide behind facts and disclaimers. But with Ethan, there was nowhere to run.

"I've been thinking about us," Annie said.

Ethan's eyebrows raised in surprise. "*You?*" He laughed. "Don't take this the wrong way, but you're not exactly an 'us' kind of woman."

"Exactly," Annie nodded, somber. "The key to cracking this case wide open is figuring out who everyone has tied themselves to. Where have they hitched their cart? To whom have they promised their loyalty?"

"And this has to do with us because... ?"

"Because I can't understand why you'd want to tie yourself to me," Annie said. She shook her head, pushing her pillow between them. "I don't have anything to offer you. All I can see are pieces and how they make up the whole. I'm terrible at just *existing*—"

"You seem to be doing a good job of it right now," Ethan laughed.

"I'm not *open*," Annie said. "I'm traumatized from the past—"

"You think I'm not traumatized?" Ethan asked, suddenly

serious. "Annie, my sister was taken too. You think that doesn't keep me up at night?"

"You've dealt with it better than me. You can function. You don't wake up shaking in the middle of the night. You're not obsessed with catching the person who did it. You didn't let it *define* you."

"Or maybe I just hide everything it's done to me because I'm determined to be the highest-functioning version of myself for one very important reason."

"What reason?"

Ethan looked at her, still daunted at Annie's inability to solve the case right in front of her. He tucked a piece of hair behind her ear.

"The reason," Ethan whispered, "Is that I tied myself to this brilliant woman a long time. And that's where my loyalty lies."

"What if I'm a bad partner for you?" Annie said, eyes stinging. "What if I can't give you the kind of relationship you deserve?"

"Then we'll end it," Ethan shrugged. "We won't be together in that way. And I'll miss out on all kinds of fun things I really enjoy." He kissed her neck to make his point. "But it won't change the fact that I'll always be here for you."

And in that moment, Annie believed he meant it. She wasn't sure how to respond. She wondered if she could ever give Ethan the kind of love he deserved. Maybe the right thing to do would be to set him free to find a person who wasn't broken. If this case had taught her nothing, it was that the person you tied yourself to could change your life forever.

There was a buzzing sound from the beside table nearest to Ethan. He grabbed his phone, plucking it from its charger to read a message.

"Interesting," he said, running a hand through his hair. "What?"

"The police received an anonymous tip. Tomorrow at noon in the lobby restaurant," he passed Annie his phone. "They want us there for the bust."

Annie read the message, committing its parts to memory almost immediately.

"Does it match your impression?" Ethan asked.

"No," Annie smiled. "But the suspects are certainly falling into the trap we set. I'm almost disappointed," she continued. "I thought they'd be more creative."

"They probably have a lot on their minds, what with you on their trail," Ethan rolled on top of her, holding himself up. "I know I'd be distracted."

He kissed her, then pulled away.

"Annie, if you don't want this— if you don't want to be *tied* to anyone— all you have to do is tell me, and I'll set you free."

Annie rested in the earnestness of his affection. All Ethan wanted was to solve the puzzle inside her head, even when she hadn't solved it herself. Annie wanted to give him an answer, but instead, she kissed him back, letting herself forget the moment.

CHAPTER TWENTY-SEVEN

ANNIE AND ETHAN waited outside *Rowling Heights*, crouched in the back of a white van that looked— from the outside— like a food truck selling tacos.

"This is the best the FBI could come up with?" Police Chief Sanchez swatted at a rogue fly that buzzed around the back of a truck.

"Nobody said the cover had to be glamorous," Ethan countered.

Annie leaned in, looking at a series of video monitors that had been stacked at the far end of the van. Each one showed a different view of the restaurant in *Rowling Heights'* lobby. On the screens, diners enjoyed their meals, and waiters passed in and out of view.

"That's our guy right there," Chief Sanchez pointed at one of the screens, singling out a man in a baseball cap reading a newspaper. "We've got another one undercover near the door."

"This is too much for a fake lead," Annie said, rolling her eyes.

"We have to take every anonymous tip seriously," Sanchez shrugged. "I would love if this were our guy. I could wrap this thing up with a pretty little bow and tell Ferdinand his son has been avenged. Then, I'd eat tacos on the beach. From a *real* truck."

"While the wrong guy rots in prison?" Annie asked.

"You get me the evidence for the right guy, and we'll go from there," Chief Sanchez shrugged.

"No," Annie said. "We need this to play out anyway. For me to be sure I'm right."

"The tip was pretty clear," Chief Sanchez hedged. "It said it was from a friend who he'd offered a confession to. They said there'd be proof in his jacket pocket. That he'd been carrying it around since he murdered Tony, as a sort of prize."

"Pretty diabolical. Doesn't line up with what I know about him. Not to mention he has no motive."

"The motive will present itself when we question him. That's how it always goes with these guys."

"He didn't do it," Annie added simply. "Still, you said you wanted to proceed—"

"There's no other choice," Ethan added. "You go on your information, and we'll move on ours."

"It's a go," Chief Sanchez said into a walkie-talkie. They waited, breathless, watching on the screens for any sign of the suspect in question. Then, he appeared:

Hathaway. He was wearing his typical grey blazer and tie, a computer bag on one shoulder. By the relaxed rhythm of his gait, Annie could tell he was clueless as to what was about to happen. He stopped at the restaurant's host stand, presumably asking to be seated. Before the waiter could show him to his seat, all hell broke loose. The undercover officer in a baseball cap rushed toward him, gun drawn. Behind him, the officer by the door pushed Hathaway's hands behind his back, clapping a pair of handcuffs over his wrist.

"You want in on the bust?" Chief Sanchez said, ushering Annie and Ethan out of the van. Bright light flooded Annie's eyes as she stumbled out of the van and rushed across the sidewalk. Her vision turned dark just as quickly as they entered the building, her eyes and mind struggling to adjust to what had just happened. They moved quickly toward the restaurant, where Hathaway was being subdued in a corner booth. Onlookers stared, and additional officers in uniform pushed citizens away from the scene.

"My lawyers!" Hathaway shouted. "They'll hear about this! Arrest without cause—"

Chief Sanchez moved toward Hathaway and pushed open his jacket, reaching into the inside pocket. She removed a gold pendant, allowing it to dangle from its chain for Annie and Ethan to view.

It was a small, gold, penguin hovering in mid-air.

"I—" Hathaway sputtered. "That shouldn't be there. It *wasn't* there this morning—"

"Do you recognize it?" Chief Sanchez asked Annie.

"It belonged to Tony," Annie confirmed. "We have photographs of him wearing it."

"Perfect," Chief Sanchez said. She turned to Hathaway. "Did you take this off him when you pushed him? You like a souvenir do you?"

"That's— not—" Hathaway's breathing quickened. He thought of his tropical fish back in the tank in his living room, and how he'd give anything to be back upstairs in the safety of his apartment. "I didn't kill him. You haven't even read me my rights!"

"Thanks for the reminder. Cadet!" Chief Sanchez called over her shoulder. A police cadet appeared out of thin air.

"Hathaway," Annie leaned closer, keeping her voice lower. "Don't worry. I know it wasn't you. This will be over soon."

Hathaway stared at her, flabbergasted at how he'd arrived in such a terrible spot. The cadet grabbed Hathaway and ushered him toward the door, reading him his rights as they went.

"You have the right to remain silent—"

The pair disappeared around the corner right as another officer arrived, whispering something in Chief Sanchez's ear.

"Really?" She smiled at him. Then, she turned to Annie and Ethan. "You're gonna want to see this."

She led them through the building's lobby, across the foyer to the display case that only days earlier had featured teapots in a whimsical Mother's Day display. Annie leaned in, looking at the case's new contents. There were photos of the residents Annie had named as suspects and a brief biography next to each one. The display featured paper cutouts in the shapes of stars and flowers, clearly crafted with joyous care.

Annie stopped at a picture of Mindy. It had been taken in the building's main coffee shop, and she was waving a hand in the air, smiling. But it was what was laying over her blouse that caught Annie's eye:

A necklace with a gold chain, featuring a small penguin at the end. It was smaller than Tony's necklace but otherwise served as an exact match.

"That's Hathaway's ex-wife, right?" Chief Sanchez asked. Annie nodded. "There's our motive," Sanchez shrugged. "Let me know if you want to take a crack at him in questioning. Looks like an easy one to break."

With that, Chief Sanchez took off, leaving Annie and Ethan to consider the mess that had been made.

"I hope for his sake we're close," Ethan said, nodding at a picture of Hathaway inside the case. Annie had never wanted to say "yes" so badly, but instead, she stared at the picture, thinking about how much she had left to prove.

CHAPTER TWENTY-EIGHT

HATHAWAY

THERE WAS a chip in the paint. Hathaway couldn't take his eyes off of it, his mind intensely focused on the shape of the chip. It was on the wall opposite where he was seated, a gouge in an otherwise seamless eggshell surface. The chip was located a few inches beneath a reflective two-way mirror, on the other side of which—Hathaway knew— police officers and detectives were watching him. But Hathaway didn't want to think about that, or about the fact he was handcuffed to a metal table, sitting on a hard, steel chair. Instead, he focused on the chip in the paint, wondering how it had happened, and deciding it looked more like a boot than the country of Italy.

"It was in your pocket," Chief Sanchez said, sliding a picture of the penguin necklace across the table. The necklace itself had been entered into evidence, no longer available to view. "You want to explain how that happened?"

"I'll wait for my lawyer," Hathaway said. He had repeated this phrase so many times in the past hour that he'd lost count. He knew it was the right answer— the only answer— in a situation like the one he'd found himself in.

He returned his gaze to the chip in the paint, making up a

story as to how it had come to be. He imagined it was made when a man— wrongly accused— suddenly discovered powers of strength, bursting out of his handcuffs and breaking through the two-way mirror toward freedom, chipping the wall in the process.

Just in case it was true, Hathaway pulled at his own handcuffs. They didn't budge. No dice.

There was a squeaking sound as the door behind Hathaway opened. He looked over his shoulder as best he could with his hands restrained, making out the lithe figure of Annie behind him. Her arms were crossed, her mouth set in a thin line.

"Hour's up," she said, apparently referencing some kind of pre-arranged agreement with Chief Sanchez. Sanchez stood, unoffended. She exited the room without another word, leaving Annie and Hathaway on their own— except for the two-way mirror, of course.

Annie moved to the table, pulling out the chair that had previously been occupied by Chief Sanchez. Hathaway glanced away from the chip in the wall, allowing his eyes to fall on the woman who had become a common sight around his apartment building.

"I didn't do it," Hathaway said.

Annie nodded in agreement. "Of course you didn't," she assured him. Hathaway's eyebrows arched in surprise. Her support was the last thing he'd expected. A wave of relief washed over him, followed by a prickling skepticism— why should she believe him?

"You don't think so?" He asked, dumbfounded.

"You didn't kill Tony Vasquez," Annie said, her tone casual, as if she were speaking to Hathaway on any regular day and not the worst day of his life. "But someone is trying to frame you for the crime. Which makes your arrest a pivotal step in gathering evidence against the true perpetrator."

"*Frame* me?" Hathaway said, his mouth dropping open.

The idea hadn't occurred to him, if only because it was the poorest of excuses. Although his specialty wasn't criminal law, Hathaway knew from his colleagues that every guilty party claimed to have been framed. He'd never considered such a cliche excuse might become his living truth, its breath just as rapid and pungent as his own. "It makes sense," he whispered, nodding. "Yes, someone must have framed me. The necklace wasn't in my jacket. I'd never have moved it—"

He froze, realizing what he'd done. The mistake he'd made was unfixable. Across the table, Annie looked immovable, her small smile neither growing nor shrinking in size. "Not to worry," she reassured Hathaway. "I know you stole the necklace. You went back to erase your fingerprints. But that was a trap I laid for you. By the time we told you we were planning on searching Tony's place for prints, we'd already taken some. They came back as yours."

Hathaway's cheeks reddened, angry that he'd fallen for such a simple ploy. Of course a Detective would never tip their hand by revealing their next course of action, unless, of course, it was in their benefit to do so. He had underestimated Annie. It was something about the ease with which she operated that had caused him to make such a fatal error. She seemed to calm, too young, and maybe, too female to be capable of strategic warfare.

"You might as well put me away now then," Hathaway said, defeated. Maybe Mindy *was* right and— without her— he was nothing but a screw-up, incapable of even the simplest tasks.

"I don't think that will be necessary," Annie said. "As a lawyer, I'm sure you know the benefits of cooperation. If you work with me to catch the real killer and I can find evidence to support my conclusion, I'm sure we can strike a deal."

"I'd like the terms up front," Hathaway countered, some small fire still within him blazing to life. "I need it in writing. Not more than a misdemeanor. No jail time."

"You're not in much of a position to negotiate," she reminded him, motioning around the room. "Your best bet isn't a piece of paper or an agreement. It's me."

Hathaway slumped, realizing the truth in her words. He wasnt much of a gambling man, but it was clear there was only one bet to be made.

"What do you want to know?"

"Why'd you take the necklace?"

Hathaway sighed. "I'd mentioned I'm in the middle of a divorce—"

"Only about one hundred times, quite angrily I might add," Annie smiled.

"Well, if you haven't noticed, and I'm sure you have... it's been quite acrimonious. There's a lot of money at stake. Money that was *mine* to start with. Mindy argues she helped grow it, but that hardly entitles her—"

"The necklace," Annie said, impatient. "Why?"

Hathaway leaned in, his eyes glinting a little the way they did when he spoke about obscure terms of law. He wasn't the world's greatest lawyer, but that didn't keep him from loving the sport of it. "There's a term in our prenuptial agreement. A carve-out."

"That says?"

"If she cheats... she gets nothing."

"Mindy was having an affair with Tony?" Annie tapped her fingers on the table, pleased. She had suspected as much, but now she had a witness account to support her claim, making the existing evidence less than circumstantial. "He's half her age."

"Disgusting, isn't it?"

"Actually, I was hoping to congratulate her," Annie laughed. "I'll have to send her a fruit basket."

"They were quiet about it, for obvious reasons, one being the age difference. She's in her late fifties. He's in his thirties.

The girls at her Pilates class wouldn't look on it kindly. But then there's the *bigger* reason—"

"The prenup. Does it still hold, even though you're separated?"

Hathaway's cheeks lifted in an uneven grin, the light hitting hard on half of his face, illuminating the damage time had done. "The clause defines cheating as extramarital sexual activity during time *married*, not separated. We are, to this day, still legally married."

"Interesting," Annie said. "And you stole the penguin necklace because—"

"Because they each got one! Tacky, but very much up Mindy's alley. Two matching bird necklaces to show their *love*. She thought I didn't see, but of course, half the building was onto them. And then I noticed her, showing up at our proceedings one day with that stupid, clumsy bird around her neck. And one day later, I saw Tony with the same charm."

"But why take the necklace?" Annie wondered aloud. "You could have just shown photographic evidence of each."

"That was my plan," Hathaway countered. "I intended to photograph his closet, say that he invited me over and I stumbled onto it. But then I saw it laying there and—"

"You were angry," Annie said.

"Maybe a little drunk, too," Hathaway admitted.

"Unlucky for you that ended up being the day Tony was murdered."

Hathaway held up his hands, which were still shackled to the table, showing off his handcuffs to demonstrate the point. "Tell me about it."

"Once you stole the necklace, what did you do with it?"

"I realized the next day how stupid I'd been," Hathaway said, images of the moments after the crime swimming in his mind's eye. "But at that point, getting rid of it might have made things worse. And then Tony showed up dead, and the stakes were raised. I realized how it all looked. So I hid it in a compartment in my kitchen. The cabinets are from the prohibition era. There's a built-in nook."

"Did anybody else know you'd placed it there?"

"No one."

"Did anyone else know about the compartment's existence?"

"Of course not," Hathaway shook his head. Then, he paused, a thought occurring to him. "Then again—"

"What?" Annie leaned in.

"The apartments were all built at the same time. Most have been updated, but not all of them. It never occurred to me, but anybody else who lived in the building might also know about the compartment, because, well—"

"Their apartment could have a hiding spot as well. Thank you," Annie said. "That's helpful. What about the morning before you went to get lunch at the restaurant? What did you do? Who did you see?"

"It was like any other morning," Hathaway shrugged. "I woke up, fed the fish, then later in the afternoon, headed downstairs to get some lunch. Mindy and I both have set days we eat there without each other. We used to go together, but now we rotate, given everything that's happened. Tuesdays are *my* days and I never miss them."

"Did you run into anyone in the hallway?"

"I bumped into Cataline going down the elevator," Hathaway offered. "And I saw Alejandro in the lobby, talking on his cell phone. I waved at him, but that was it. Next thing I knew, I was ambushed by cops, and now I'm here. Talking to you." He said the last sentence with resigned disappointment like he'd won the worst prize at the county fair.

"Thank you," Annie said. "This has been helpful."

She stood, turning to exit the room. "That's it?" Hathaway asked. He wished he had something more to offer. Desperation churned in his stomach. He needed to get out of here. He couldn't stay here. Not him. The son of an influential family. This wasn't supposed to be his destiny. It was as if he'd woken up in the wrong timeline, in somebody's else's story. "Is there anything else I can do?"

"Don't worry," Annie said, her eyes wide with sympathy. "We'll be in touch. It won't be long, now. Just a few more loose ends to tie up." She paused, looking at something across the room near the two-way mirror.

"It looks like Italy, doesn't it?"

For a moment, the comment didn't register, and Hathaway had no idea what she was referencing. Then, he followed Annie's gaze to the paint chip, still stick in the wall like a scar on an otherwise seamless face.

"The chip in the paint," she explained. "You were looking at it earlier. Personally, it reminds me of Italy."

The door shut softly behind her, and all at once, Hathaway was alone.

CHAPTER TWENTY-NINE

CAR DOORS SLAMMED as Annie and Ethan slipped themselves into the Jeep Cherokee he'd rented for the duration of their stay on the West Coast. They buckled their seatbelts, neither one of them wanting to say what they were thinking or guess at the conclusion of the other.

"Chief Sanchez said she's got a lead on our letter," Ethan said, matter of fact.

"Did she say who? Or where?" Annie's voice raised an octave, hopeful.

"She didn't give me any details. She's withholding, I think, until we close this thing out. Some friend you've got there."

"Define friend," Annie sighed.

"Doesn't look good for Hathaway," Ethan let out a low whistle.

"We can save him," Annie answered, rolling down her window. She was stationed passenger side, like she usually was when Ethan drove. He knew she hated driving with a passion. The signs. The noises. Because her mind was focused on minor details, driving— for Annie— felt like a technicolor whirl of too much information. Whenever she could avoid the task and rely instead on public transportation, she chose the latter.

Ethan revved the engine, fixing the rearview mirror. "What's the plan?"

"Three more interviews," Annie said. "I'm three interviews away from being able to present my findings. Assuming they all pan out the way I hope they will."

"To *Rowling Heights* it is," Ethan said, backing the car out just a little too quickly. He loved the feeling of another case resolved. When Annie was close to a conclusion, Ethan felt the adrenaline rush of having helped her make the world just a little bit fairer. A little bit more *just.*

They made their way down the pike, turning out into traffic. Ethan inhaled, glancing sideways at Annie like he couldn't help himself. She was at her most beautiful when she was about to solve a case. Something about the riddle in her eyes got him— every time.

"Did you think anymore," he asked, "about the question I asked you the other night?"

Annie didn't answer. She was chewing on her fingernails, still considering the ways her investigation could be resolved. She looked up at him, surprised.

"About whether or not you want to be tied together?" Ethan clarified. "You didn't give me a clear yes or no."

"After the case?" Annie said, determined not to let her personal life muddy the waters of her brain, which were already at high- tide, brimming with all the information she could hold.

"No problem," Ethan conceded. "I'll hold you to it. But, Annie?"

"Yes."

"At the risk of pointing out something you haven't considered, as far as being tied together goes— between what happened when we were kids, and our siblings and the cases were solving, and what we're *doing* out here, together, and everything we've been through. Annie, don't you see?"

She didn't.

"Fuck the question of whether or not we want to be tied together. Annie, as far as I'm concerned— look around. We already are."

Annie couldn't help it. She smiled at him, then suddenly burst out laughing. He joined her, taking her hand in his, the two of them cruising down a coastal highway, windows wide open like they weren't afraid of the world.

CHAPTER THIRTY

MINDY

MINDY'S APARTMENT was decorated in protest. Everything about the space was planned to offer a direct contrast to the apartment she'd shared with Hathaway. Where Hathaway's home featured dark Mahogany siding, Mindy had painted the original wood paneling in her new apartment a sleek, bright white. The furniture she'd shared with Hathaway was a masculine brown leather, but Mindy's new couches were made from canvas in a feminine, pink shade. In Hathaway's apartment, the walls were devoid of any art, but in Mindy's new place, brightly-colored prints— and even some outrageously expensive originals— hung on the walls. A facsimile of the Andy Warhol Campbell's soup piece. A Yayoi Kasuma recreation, purchased from a dealer downtown. All of it was intended to symbolize Mindy's newfound freedom— her liberation from the confining marriage that had only taken from her and had never given.

Today, however, the freedom she'd been enjoying was losing its sheen.

"We should never have started the affair in the first place," she said, wiping her nose. She was seated on one of her custom-made couches, across from Annie and Ethan, who stared back at her with sympathy. "Hathaway and I were separated at the time," she said, dabbing at her face with a tissue. "You should know that."

"Why did you hide it?" Annie asked.

"I think you know why," Mindy rolled her eyes.

"But I'd like to confirm the story."

"There's a clause in the prenup that cheating means I get nothing. And make no mistake, I *earned* that money," she leaned forward, her eyes suddenly blazing. "Hathaway is a man born with everything, but he never knew what to do with it. I helped him avoid total ruin. I made him what he is today. Without me, the man can barely pack a lunch for himself." She paused, taking a rattling inhale, her eyes watering as she thought of Tony. "Tony was different. He was young, but he wanted things out of life. He didn't have it all figured out—"

"Most of the descriptions we've gathered paint Tony as a little adrift," Annie offered.

"Yes," Mindy agreed. "He was a bit lost, but the difference was that he appreciated *me*. He made me feel like I was the only woman in the room. He was grateful for what I brought to his life. With Tony, I wasn't invisible."

"So you kept your relationship a secret because of the prenup?"

"It wasn't just that," Mindy said. "Our age difference was, well, a little embarrassing. When a man dates a younger woman no one bats an eye, but I knew what people would say about me if my relationship with Tony became news in the building. They'd call me a cougar. Whisper behind my back. Hedge bets on how long it would be before he cheated on me. I'd been going through so much, what with the divorce— I didn't think I could handle the speculation. Even though my marriage to Hathaway wasn't everything I'd hoped, I was still... grieving. Even when something's awful, when it's over, we still grieve. Do you know what I mean?"

Annie nodded. "Yes, I believe I do."

"And now— now that Tony's gone—" a sob escaped from Mindy's throat, "— I've been grieving all over again. But silently, and on my own. I've wanted to reach out to his father, but I worry what he would think of an older woman dating his son—"

"We've met Ferdinand," Ethan offered. "I'm sure he'd like to know." He glanced at Annie, whose expression said she *wasn't* so sure. Still, Ethan pressed on. "We can get you his contact information once the investigation is over if you'd like."

Mindy blew her nose into a tissue. "That would mean everything. Thank you." She paused, noticing a lightness in her chest. "It feels good to get this out in the open. I've been mourning this loss all alone. Talking about it— helps." She looked at Annie and Ethan, the realization that they were solely responsible for avenging the man she loved suddenly dawning on her. Her mouth dropped open, horrified. "I lied to you," she said. "I should've told you the truth about Tony and me much earlier. But I kept it to myself because it had become such a habit to hide it. I should've said— you don't think— did the fact I kept this a secret impact the investigation? I *do* want to see him avenged. I only thought— I thought our relationship wasn't relevant. Wouldn't *mean* anything—"

"It does mean something," Annie offered. "But you can make it right, today."

Mindy nodded. Then, she offered, resigned:

"Hathaway didn't kill Tony. I say that out of love for Tony, not in defense of Hathaway. I want to see the right person arrested for Tony's murder, and I can tell you—Hathaway doesn't have it in him. He's not a killer."

"I agree," Annie said. "But now I need evidence to prove it. It's not looking good for Hathaway. He went back to get the necklace—"

Mindy waved a hand in the air. She reached under her blouse and pulled out a charm that was hiding beneath the silk. A gold penguin dangled from the chain. "A silly thing. Tony and I bought them at a jewelry store in the Gaslamp District. He said penguins were a bit like our love." Her lower lip trembled at the memory. "They're awkward birds. Nobody quite understands them. They don't really make sense, do they? A bird that can't fly. But they mate for life. Did you know that?" She waited for Ethan or Annie to answer, but neither one offered confirmation. "It's true. Penguins mate for life. They pick one partner who they love, and they never mate again." Tears streamed down her cheeks at the thought. "He was my penguin."

"Why would Hathaway want Tony's necklace?"

"Hathaway is astoundingly good at coming up with bad ideas," Mindy sighed. "It's one of his only talents. He'd probably had one too many drinks and thought stealing the necklace was some kind of revenge. Or he thought he'd use it against me in the divorce as evidence of my relationship with Tony. Stupid. Childish. That's Hathaway. But a murderer? No."

"Who do you think *would* have killed Tony," Annie asked. "Did he have any enemies?"

"Not one," Mindy said. "The man was an angel. Everyone loved him," she paused, considering. "But— a few weeks before it happened, Tony *did* say that his father had received a strange, anonymous offer on the apartment. Someone had wanted the penthouse in particular, and they were relentless. Calls emails. A willingness to lease for three years, all cash, upfront. At one point, Tony thought about saying "yes" and taking the money to start his own business. But he would have had nowhere to live. I would have offered that he move in with me— I *should* have—" Mindy said, voice trembling. "But until the damn divorce proceedings finished, I couldn't."

"Did Tony seem afraid at all in the days before he died?"

"No," Mindy said. "If anything, he seemed hopeful about the future. He was a little tormented over whether he should take the offer from this anonymous source, but once he firmly decided to stay in the building, he seemed relieved. He wanted to stay near me," she added. "He told me he had a great home, a great girlfriend, and his life was finally coming together. Like I said— he made me feel appreciated."

"One final question," Annie said. She grabbed her phone and scrolled through the photos app, landing on a picture of the lobby display case. She pinched in with two fingers, zooming in before passing the phone to Mindy. "That picture of you that's in the display case. Who took it?"

Mindy squinted, staring at the photo of herself. She was standing in the lobby, smiling, the penguin necklace fully visible over her shirt.

"That's easy," she said. "I remember that day well. I was downstairs complaining about Hathaway and was made to feel so lucky to live in a building where people cared. She stopped me. She told me everything was going to be okay and that they were there for me."

"Who?" Anni asked.

There was a long pause, and then Mindy said the word that Annie had been hoping for:

"*Cataline.*"

CHAPTER THIRTY-ONE

ALFRED

ALFRED HAD the feeling something very bad was happening.

He was holed up in his office— as he usually was this time of day—surrounded by repair requests that needed answering, and things that needed doing. But what made this moment different was the presence of the two detectives—Annie and Ethan—standing in his doorway, looking at him like they knew a secret that he'd been hiding.

Alfred's heart pounded in his chest, its reverberations so loud that he couldn't make out what Annie had just been saying.

"The tapes," she reiterated, her voice far away. "Alfred, did you understand me? I'm going to need to talk to you about the tapes again."

The world stopped spinning, its pieces coming into sharp relief. Colors seemed brighter, and edges looked sharper. Alfred snapped back into the moment. He knew what he had to do.

"Come in then," he said. "And close the door behind you."

Annie and Ethan did as they were instructed, closing the

door and making themselves comfortable on a couple of folding chairs they found leaning against the back wall.

"What brought you back?" Alfred asked, defeated. He glanced at the bank of monitors on his desk, each of them broadcasting a chunky image from the barely-operational security cameras he'd installed. He regretted putting the entire system into place. It had brought him nothing but trouble, and now, trouble had come home to roost.

"To be honest, Alfred, my mind never really left you," Annie said, a smile on her face. "A man like you— so dedicated to the building that it's his primary purpose in life— somehow allows the cameras to malfunction on the night a resident is murdered. Difficult to believe, isn't it? Hardly matches who I know you to be— or the man I believe you are."

"I'm not a born liar," Alfred said, shaking his head. "Never have been."

"And then, I had to ask myself... If Alfred deleted the footage, why? Who was he protecting? And something Ferdinand told me about the building stuck with me. It was something he said when we started this investigation. He told me you have to look at where a person's loyalties lie. Who have they tied themselves to? Wagon, meet horse—" Annie placed her left hand in the air to represent the wagon, and her right hand in the air to represent the horse. "So, Alfred, I'm wondering who you hitched your wagon to."

Alfred inhaled, thinking about his options. "I could decline to say a word and you couldn't prove anything. The footage is gone. There's nothing you can do about it."

"That's true," Annie said, leaning back in her chair as if looking for the solution to a very big problem. "And yet, I think you'll choose to tell me anyway."

"Why's that?"

"Because *I* believe your wagon is hitched to the building." Annie scooted to the edge of her chair, resting her elbows on her thighs so she could better stare into Alfred's eyes. "I believe that, much like Ethan and me, you've tied yourself to a cause that's bigger than *you*. And while you might love one individual person, your love for that cause is greater. And that cause— is *Rowling Heights*. I don't have to tell you what an unsolved case like this means for the building. In two years, this place will become a ghost town. The site of a murder. Associated with gore instead of luster. You heard what happened to the Smithinson Building in Los Angeles?"

Alfred nodded. There was a similar complex up north that used to be the jewel of the neighborhood. But after a gruesome crime was committed in the lobby, it became fodder for folklore— an empty apartment building forced to offer short-term rentals to YouTubers and Ghosthunters.

"You wouldn't want that to happen to *Rowling Heights*, would you? This place deserves better than that. This building, and the people in it, are special."

Alfred considered. He knew what he'd done was wrong. Maybe it was time to make amends.

"And I have your word you'll look out for the interests of the building?"

"You have my word I'll solve the case, which I believe supports the interests of the building."

"It wasn't relevant," Alfred said, shaking his head. "I saw the footage and panicked, so I deleted it. But I knew it wasn't relevant to the case. Because neither one of them would ever hurt Tony."

"What did you see on the footage?" Annie asked.

Alfred let out a big sigh, his shoulders sagging with the weight of what he was about to reveal. "There was a package outside Tony's door the night he died. The mail gets sorted that way. We hand deliver packages whenever we can, especially since, you know the mail room debacle and the situation with the roof."

"There was a package outside his door," Annie encouraged.

"And, well, when I was reviewing the security camera footage for that night, I happened to notice something strange. Somebody came and took the package from outside Tony's door. If I didn't know this person better, I'd say it was — *stealing*."

"Who took the package?"

There was a long pause, and then— too far down the road to make a detour— Alfred finally offered up the truth:

"Cataline's son. Mario."

"Mario took the package," Annie confirmed. "And then what?"

"Nothing," Alfred shrugged. "He left. Went down the elevator. He didn't kill him. I know Mario well, and the boy's a good kid." Alfred spoke with increasing speed, his words tumbling out one after the other. "I worried he'd be blamed for the strange mail activity. So many ways for the young man to get into trouble. He didn't do a thing. He was *friends* with Tony. They'd play video games together. But I worried it looked suspicious and I just couldn't stand to see him implicated—"

"What about *after* that? Did you see anyone come or go?"

Alfred blanched. The color drained from his face. A terrible idea was nesting in his brain— one he had considered until this very moment. "After?"

"You kept watching the footage, of course. After Mario took the package, there must have been *someone* who came up the elevator shaft. That person could very well be the one who murdered Tony."

Alfred's mouth dropped open, his expression unreadable. Then, he sputtered, "*After*— I didn't— I didn't keep watching — I didn't *think*..."

Ethan shook his ahead, attempting to hide his frustration.

"You didn't think to keep watching the footage?" Ethan exclaimed, aghast.

Alfred threw his hands in the air. "I'm not a detective! This isn't— those cameras were just there to make the residents feel safer." He dropped his hands, coming to terms with what he'd done. "As soon as I saw Mario on that tape, all I could think about was deleting the footage. I was so panicked, so worried for him and Cataline that I erased it without a second thought." The room spun again. Alfred clutched the edge of his chair as if to keep from falling. "If I'd kept watching, we would know who the killer is. It's my fault, I've ruined it all for Tony. For Ferdinand—"

"Not quite," Annie smiled, patting him on his arm. "I know who the killer is. And soon enough, you will, too."

She rose, stretching her arms to the sky like she'd had a long day and could use a nap, but otherwise had nothing else to be concerned about. Ethan followed her, and the moved toward the door to exit. But before they left, Annie turned to Alfred one more time.

"Who made you redo the display case in the lobby? I thought the teapots were lovely. Was sad to see them go."

There was a long pause, and then Alfred answered: "Cataline."

Annie smiled, thrilled to see her suspicions were lining up with the facts.

"For what it's worth, Alfred," she said. "I think you hitched your wagon to the right horse. You have to be careful who you tie yourself to, nowadays."

"Which horse did I choose?" Alfred asked.

"You chose the building. *Rowling Heights.* A cause much bigger than any one person. You have my respect for that," Annie told him.

She left, Ethan on her trail, and the door shut softly behind them. Alfred felt like all the air had exited the room as he considered which wagon was his, and whether the horse he'd chosen was the correct one.

CHAPTER THIRTY-TWO

MONTANA

MONTANA LEANED an arm against the back of his chair, taking another puff of his cigarette. He was seated outside his favorite dive bar, located just a couple blocks away from *Rowling Heights.* He'd intentionally chosen a section of the bar that was positioned outside the building under a cabana. His table blocked the sidewalk, and every now and then a pedestrian passing by would wave a hand in front of their nose, trying to disperse the cloud of smoke Montana was creating. Montana didn't care. He had every right to live his best life. If it bothered anyone else, they could walk around him.

"Don't tell me you mind it also?" Montana asked his companions for the evening, holding up his cigarette for reference. On the other side of the table, Annie and Ethan didn't offer any objection.

"It's your night," Annie said, serious. "We're the ones interrupting it. Do whatever you need."

Montana nodded. He liked her attitude. "Thought we wrapped this up last time. Sounds like that Hathaway character is the one they're looking at. It's been all over the news." He glanced at a television screen inside that was mounted over the bar. Hathaway's face flashed across the screen in an insert over the TV reporter's shoulder. The apprehending of a suspect in the Vasquez murder was the biggest news San Diego had seen in months.

"Perhaps," Annie said. "But we still need to gather the correct evidence. To help them make a strong case against him." She was lying, but she did it so well that Montana didn't pick up on the deception.

"Ask away. Anything I can do to help."

"Certainly," Annie agreed. "But before we start on the case, I just have to ask… I've looked into your record as a DHS agent. Incredible career."

"You looking for a change?" Montana grimaced.

"Not me," Annie smiled. "But Ethan here. He's done with the FBI. Long hours. Little pay. He still wants to be in the action but, you know, he's ready to get out."

Ethan tried to cover his smirk. Annie loved doing this to him. She used him as a pawn on the chessboard that was her negotiation. By now, he'd grown used to it. Like an improv performer trained to say "yes-and," Ethan had learned to agree with whatever Annie said just to keep the ball rolling.

"You've had enough then, huh?" Montana asked Ethan, eyes searching his reaction.

"Yes," Ethan said. "That's me. So ready for change. I'm a big change-it-up kind of guy."

"Not many people have the stomach for our kind of work," Montana leaned back in his chair, flinging his finished cigarette onto the cement.

"Sure," Ethan rolled his eyes. "My employment with the FBI could hardly be considered preparation for the challenge of the DHS."

Annie kicked Ethan under the table. In a stroke of good fortune, Montana didn't seem to pick on the sarcasm in Ethan's tone.

"People think all alphabets are the same, but the DHS

takes a special breed," Montana said. "You know what's toughest about it?" He leaned in, crossing his arms. "After you've been there long enough, you start to realize there ain't no good guys or bad guys. There's just power. The entire idea of a border— what is that anyway? Something made by people who say, 'Hey, this is ours.' It's tribalism. Organized government isn't that much different from a cartel. It's all just people with strength and money looking for ways to use both."

"You don't see much difference between a government and a cartel?" Annie asked, her tone pleasant.

"Do you?"

"One is elected by the people to work on their behalf in a service capacity," Annie offered. "The other imposes itself on the people through violence."

"Sure," Montanan shrugged. "The cartel uses physical violence. But the government— *our* government— if you don't think they use violence too, you ain't payin' attention."

"Can you give me an example?" Annie asked.

"Kids in cages. No health insurance. It's hard as anything to make a dime, give a man the pride of providing for his family. Hell, we have veterans sleeping on the sidewalk. Not all violence is physical."

Annie soaked in his words like she was looking for some deeper meaning, her eyes crinkling at every change of inflection in his voice. She leaned back, satisfied with whatever she had found in the dark pool of his eyes.

"Is that important to you? The ability to provide for a family."

"Don't have one," Montana answered. "But the idea of one. That matters."

Annie stared at the horizon. From where they were sitting, the ocean was fully visible. A line formed in the place where the sea met the sky, two different shades of blue fighting for dominance in the distance. "You see the cartel and the government as different sides of the same coin."

"That's just been my experience," Montana shrugged. "You may see it different."

"Yes," Annie said. "So much of what we do relies on perception." She looked back at the horizon, focusing on a brown patch of land that jutted out into the harbor. The lighthouse was fully visible, its stone facade reaching for the sky. Beside it, the DHS building rested on a rocky incline, its brick exterior offering a solid, unwavering commentary on who was welcome, here, and who wasn't. The DHS boats were anchored near the pier, currently unused but lined up like soldiers awaiting further orders. At a moment's notice, they could spring into action. They were always ready. Always waiting.

"Funny," Annie said, pointing at the DHS building. "You can just make out the DHS building from here, but the boats are blocked from view. Not too many places you can see them, except from *Rowling Heights*. Does it bother you, seeing your workplace from your home?"

"Doesn't bother me," Montana said. "Can't see it from my apartment. Or form any others."

Annie bristled. A still, quiet feeling settled over the table as she scanned Montana up and down. "Except one," she said. If her point bothered Montana, he didn't let it show. "Is there any other station where the DHS boats launch?"

"No," Montana answered. "Not within twenty miles, at least."

"So every DHS-branded boat must make its journey by leaving *that* location?" Annie pointed across the harbor.

"Guess so," Montana said.

"And when are the boats most often utilized? What kind of instance would call for them to launch?"

"Drug smuggling," Montana answered. "Any DHS agent

would tell you as much. But I have a feeling you already knew that."

"I ask about plenty of things I already know," Annie countered. "On the off chance, perhaps, that I'm wrong."

"Well, in this case, you aren't wrong," Montana said. "It's always drugs coming this way over the border. Drugs, or people. They pack 'em the same way. Shove them into tiny boats and try to sneak in by staying far enough out at sea. Then, when they're close enough, they pull up to the shore like they've always been here. Drugs and people. That's when they launch the boats. That's what comes over the border in our direction. The other way, from the US to Mexico, it's guns." He reached into the pocket of his coat, removing his cigarettes. Camels. He pulled out another smoke, flicking his lighter to life so that the end burned red. "Funny isn't it? We pick at our own problems. The guns go over the border and the cartels get 'em, and they use 'em to take over entire cities. Then, they send us drugs and people. The whole thing is a mess." He exhaled a cloud of smoke.

"You're not the only person in the building who smokes," Annie said.

"If you want to ask about someone in particular, you might as well do it. Don't beat around the bush."

"Cataline," Annie said. "Does she smoke? I assume you might've seen her yourself, as someone who steps outside to engage in such a hobby."

"I might've seen her smoke," Montana said. "Also might've been someone else. Not sure."

"Do you know what brand?"

"Couldn't say," Montana responded, his expression indicating that he knew, but didn't want to disclose.

"Thank you for your time," Annie said, shaking his hand. "You'll be hearing from us."

Montana held onto her hand a little too long, and there seemed to be a silent understanding between the two of them. "When?" he asked. His voice was quiet, and there was a low, resigned timber to it. It was the kind of tone reserved for weddings and anniversaries. The sort of contemplative, limitless depth that came when questioning the meaning of life, or the permanence of love— not a simple goodbye.

"Sooner than you'd like, I imagine."

Annie walked off into the distance, Ethan on her heel. Montana watched them, thinking about how they looked so right together. The two of them matching their strides to the same timing, the same rhythm. They bobbed away like those DHS boats on the horizon, a unified front that was poised to take action at any moment. They gave Montana the impression they were only waiting for the command.

He considered, then pulled a cell phone out of his pocket. He hit one button to speed dial his most-used number, then waited until the ringing stopped and he heard breathing on the other end.

"It's happening," he said into the receiver. "You're gonna have to get me out."

There was a long pause while Montana waited. The person on the other line offered no assurances. Silence filled the air.

"You said you'd take care of your own," Montana pushed. His words were met with nothing but static on the other line. Montana's heart raced. There was a jostling sound, and for a moment, he thought he might hear the words he'd been hoping for, but then—

The line went dead.

Montana slipped the phone back into his pocket, wondering at the mess he'd made of his own life. He rested his arms on the metal table in front of him, the cold surface a shock against his skin. The scent of the cigarette he was holding hung heavy in the air, and he wondered if it wouldn't be his last. He inhaled—deep—memories of how he'd arrived at his current predicament playing on repeat.

Life was a series of choices— a sequence of on-ramps and off-ramps connected to different people, some of whom would lead you home, and others who only took you further away from yourself. The destination a man arrived at was all about who he followed— who he tied himself to.

And Montana had a knack for picking the wrong people.

CHAPTER THIRTY-THREE

CATALINE

CATALINE WAS under the strange impression that she was watching herself from outside her own body. She was seated on the couch in the living room of her apartment, Annie and Ethan across from her. Annie flipped through a file, referencing something on the page, but Cataline could barely hear her. She noted the familiar objects in the room— the vase she'd found at a flea market ten years ago, the shag carpet her best friend had given her when she'd left San Diego behind— but all of them looked foreign as if they belonged to someone else. Cataline was struck by the sudden urge to hug her son, as she often did when she felt out of sorts, but reminded herself that Mario was at school and that he was safe. That was all that mattered. The thought of her child snapped Cataline back into her body, and suddenly she was more awake and alert than she had ever been. An instinct flooded her form— one both old and new— whispering the same command over and over again. *Survive.* She had to do whatever she could to get through this interview. For Mario's sake.

"A package?" Cataline asked, noticing the way the air flooded her lungs. She brought a finger to her mouth, tapping her bottom lip like an old man plucking his beard in an attempt to suggest a bad memory. "Mario hasn't gotten any packages recently."

"It wasn't sent to Mario," Annie continued, a pleasant smile crossing her face. "It was sent to Tony."

"That doesn't make any sense—"

"Of course it doesn't," Annie shrugged. "Not to me. But I think you know *exactly* why Mario used Tony's address to receive a package. He didn't send it to his own home because it was something you wouldn't approve of. Isn't that right?"

"Well, I—"

"Mario and Tony were friends. They shared a love of video games. He told Tony he needed a favor and Tony agreed."

"And what evidence do you have of this?" Cataline asked, suddenly business-like.

"Alfred told us what was on the tape," Annie said. "He saw Mario pick up the package outside Tony's door. He deleted the footage to protect him because he loves Mario. And he loves you. He trusts you both. He was worried Mario would be implicated in the package fraud that was circulating the building. He didn't want you to lose your job. Not to mention the risk of Mario being implicated in Tony's murder—"

"Mario's a *child*," Cataline whispered. "*Un niño*. He would never hurt anyone."

"I agree. That's why I need you to tell me what was in that package," Annie said. "I believe it will exonerate Mario."

Cataline chewed on the inside of her cheek. She needed to play this moment the right way. If she made one wrong turn, her son's future might be destroyed.

"We're trying to help you," Ethan added.

"Help me?" Cataline laughed. "The police have a perfectly good suspect in custody."

"You and I both know Hathaway didn't do this," Annie

said. "And I have evidence to support that fact. Frankly, the evidence is leading me somewhere else. They'll release Hathaway by next week, and when all the press uproar is done, they'll be hungry to find the right person." Annie paused, letting the moment sink in. "There's no way to escape. Not when Ferdinand won't let the investigation die. You know he'll push forever. Because he loved his son just as much as you love yours."

Cataline's heart ached at the thought of Ferdinand. She considered how kind he'd been when he gave her the job. She wanted to cry for him— and for Tony— but she held back the tears and tried instead to focus on her next move. She'd been trapped for so many years that today's predicament didn't feel any different. Impossible decisions. The weight of the world. This was all Cataline had ever known.

Cataline considered the possibilities of what she might say. But every possible answer led to a negative outcome. Finally, she settled on the least objectionable choice.

"I can show you," she said. She stood, walking to the kitchen and removing the box from the top cabinet. She emptied its contents, carrying the prize back to the detectives and dropping it on the table. Annie and Ethan leaned over to examine the item.

"A DNA test?" Ethan asked.

"A genealogy kit," Annie correct him. "Mario wasn't just looking to see his ancestry. He wanted to find relatives."

"Yes," Cataline confirmed. "I didn't know he'd ordered it."

"Why wouldn't he tell you that?" Ethan asked.

"Because when he asks me about his other family, I never answer. Sometimes, I even get angry," Cataline said. Suddenly, the tears that she'd been fighting came, spilling onto her cheeks, each one heavy with regret. "The thing Mario doesn't know is that our family is dangerous." She swallowed hard. "Growing up, I didn't know my family was different. Until I saw the guns in the garage. And my father's friends with their amo—"

"Your family is part of a cartel?"

"Not just any cartel," Cataline answered. "The Sinaloa Cartel. *Cártel de Sinaloa*, the Blood Alliance."

"They operate differently from other cartels," Ethan said to Annie. "FBI's got men on the inside, and we know they go for the hierarchical structure. They operate as a series of independent clusters working together. Lot of different leaders high up."

"Marriage and family matter," Cataline added. "They use bloodlines to create connections. That's why I didn't want Mario to do the genealogy test. What if he goes on this website—" she picked up the box, pointing to a URL on the back, "— and connects with a distant relative, leading the cartel straight to us?"

"Your father must have been high up, then, if you're worried about retribution?" Ethan asked.

"It took me some time to understand," Cataline nodded. She remembered the home she'd grown up in. Tall gates made of iron that stretched toward the sky, flowered plants weaving throughout their ranks. A home secured against any enemy. Armed guards outside the compound, ensuring their safety. As a child, Cataline had wanted for nothing. But as she'd grown, she realized that her life had come with a price. "I left because they wanted me to marry a member of the cartel to connect our two families. I realized my life would never change. I learned the cost of my position in the world. I didn't want it anymore if it hurt people. I had a cousin who helped me get across the border." Cataline reached for the crucifix she wore around her neck. "With God's protection, I made it here."

"Did anyone from the cartel come looking for you?"

"I changed my name," Cataline said. "But I am sure they were looking."

"And Mario?" Annie asked.

"What about him?"

"Who's his father?" Annie paused. "I assume, like any child, he's most interested in finding his parent. This isn't only about extended family. It's about finding his Dad."

Cataline clutched the edge of the sofa. "There was a man who helped me cross the border. I met him on my way. He was kind to me." Cataline remembered the night she met Mario's father, so many years ago. The air was warm, and the crickets were singing. He'd found her— in the back of that pickup truck, no seat belt in sight— and in an instant, worlds collided. "I think I loved him, but it— it didn't matter. It would never have worked."

"Why?" Annie said.

"For the same reason anything doesn't work. We were on different paths. Life has a way of bringing you back to what you tried to avoid, doesn't it?"

Annie nodded, thinking about how many times a case she'd worked had reminded her of the loss of her brother when she was a teenager. Life did have a way of forcing you to face the things you tried to run away from.

"Why make me relive this?" Cataline asked, suddenly angry. She stood, grabbing the DNA kit off the table and tossing it in the trashcan. "Do you have what you need? Are my son and I cleared, in your eyes?"

"I know it's difficult," Annie offered. "But we have to turn over every stone—"

"You have no idea," Cataline said. "You don't know what I've had to say 'no' to. The things they wanted me to do. It would have been easy to stay with them. My life would have been handed to me. But I did what was difficult and fled, to my own detriment. And now to my son's. I left because I wanted to lead a good life." Tears streamed down Cataline's face. She walked toward the windows in the living room, looking out across the harbor. Boats bobbed in the distance, their sails an invitation to start again somewhere else. "Once you've tied yourself to someone, it's so hard to break the bond. Even when you know you should. I just want to do what is right," Cataline said, her voice cracking. She turned, staring at Annie and Ethan. "Why is it so hard? To do what is right?"

Annie moved to the windows, standing shoulder-to-shoulder with Cataline. "You don't have a view of the DHS building," Annie said, her comment abruptly aloof in the face of Cataline's emotion.

"The what?" Cataline asked.

"Just tying up loose ends," Annie said. "I shouldn't have said anything at all. I'm sorry, for what you've been through." She leaned in, placing an arm on Cataline's shoulder. The motion appeared genuine, as if she regretted what she'd put the woman through. "Nobody wants to hurt you, and certainly not Mario. We just want justice for Tony."

Cataline nodded, pulling back and drying her eyes on the edge of her sleeve.

"I do have to ask," Annie said. "That's an interesting perfume you wear. It's strong."

"Yes," Cataline answered. "Patchouli oil."

"Covers quite a multitude of sins," Annie said. "Even cigarette smoke."

There was a long pause. Cataline offered no denial, but then, the silence was too great, and the room seemed to need filling.

"We all have our vices," Cataline finally said.

"Marlboros," Annie answered. "That's what you smoke?"

Cataline's eyebrows arched in surprise. She wasn't sure how Annie could know such a thing. Annie didn't miss the confirmation in her eyes.

"We're done," Annie said, turning toward Ethan. "The case is closed." She crossed toward him, leaving Cataline alone by the windows, looking out at the harbor. She appeared to be frozen in time, her chest moving up and down with each breath, her eyelashes closing with each blink, but otherwise—her form stayed still as a statue.

Annie grabbed her bag, then announced to the room as if it were any ordinary day:

"I know who killed Tony Vasquez."

CHAPTER THIRTY-FOUR

ALFRED

ALFRED SAT at the small desk in his office, holding the receiver on a landline telephone. The phone had been at *Rowling Heights* almost as long as Alfred, and he'd insisted on keeping a landline operating despite the more convenient changes in technology. Something about a desktop phone made Alfred feel secure, like he knew where he belonged and who he belonged to. The residents could always call down with problems. They could always reach him.

"Yes," Alfred said into the phone, his voice awash with a tone of surprise. "I'll let Ferdinand know. And you're sure you want everyone present?"

A voice on the other line offered affirmation. It was the detective, Annie, claiming that she had solved the case. She'd requested a meeting with all the suspects and was trusting Alfred to bring them together at the same time.

"No, I won't tell them what it's regarding," Alfred assured her. "I can understand why you'd want to keep it private, what with the flight risk. Yes, of course. No, no— I'm quite sure I can think of a reason that will guarantee their presence. An excuse, if you will. It might require me to lie, but—"

Annie's voice on the other end of the line was a soothing flow of assurances.

"I agree. It's for a good cause. Yes... for Tony."

Alfred nodded, then hung up the phone. He took a deep breath, convinced of what he had to do. He rummaged through a filing box underneath the desk, stopping when he'd found what he was looking for. He removed a crumpled sheet of paper and smoothed it flat on his desk.

It was a list of the names of every suspect in the case.

He stared at it for a minute as if committing it to memory, then reached for a rolodex on the desk's edge. He flipped to the first card and started to dial.

CHAPTER THIRTY-FIVE

ALEJANDRO

ALEJANDRO WAS PILING a stack of clothing into a metal trashcan when the call came. He rushed to cell phone, almost as if he'd been expecting someone important.

"Hello?" he said into the receiver. Alfred's voice echoed from the other end, a muffled, familiar drawl.

"About my Tequila?" Alejandro brightened. He knew it was important to have close friends, even when those friends were part of the wait staff. Alejandro felt a sudden rush of gratitude toward himself that he'd always treated Alfred with dignity and care. Or, at least, been cordial. But that was the same thing. "Well, of course, I would love to speak to them. When you say 'investor,' how deep might their funds go?"

Alfred's voice murmured a brief answer on the other end of the line. Alejandro let out a low whistle. "Yes," he said, "I think that would be just enough to allow us to expand internationally."

He paced around the living room, his feet carving a pattern into the rug. "Tomorrow night at 5 p.m.? In the conference room. Yes, yes, I'll be there. And Alfred? *Gracias por tu ayuda.*"

Alejandro hung up the phone and threw a fist into the air,

unable to believe his incredible luck. Here he'd been worried about being implicated in the package scandal, and in fact, the very man who might have turned him in was offering him a connection to an investor. Alejandro knew he'd been right in his life strategy— it paid to have friends.

Now, all that was left to do was to destroy the evidence of his previous, slightly less legal business endeavor. Just in case the detectives weren't as friendly as they'd appeared, he tossed another leather jack into the trashcan. Then, he hauled the can onto his balcony. It was slightly shorter than the barrier, which made Alejandro confident no one could see it from the street. He pulled a lighter out of a storage compartment on the side of the grill he kept outside, then clicked the end. He lit the cuff of a sleeve, and within seconds, the whole can went up in flames.

Alejandro felt he'd dodged a bullet. This was his chance to start fresh.

CHAPTER THIRTY-SIX

MINDY

MINDY WAS WATCHING her favorite soap opera when she noticed her cell phone vibrating on the table. She normally wouldn't answer in the middle of an episode, but when she saw Alfred's name on the caller ID, she picked up at once. Alfred was such a dear, and was practically her personal assistant, what with how often he helped her with a myriad of requests.

"Alfred?" Mindy asked. "Oh no, that's fine. Of course I can talk. Not doing anything important at all—"

She nodded her head along to the hum of Alfred's voice on the other end. "Really? Typically my attorney would call me directly. Oh, he said it didn't go through? Well, my service here *is* atrocious. Yes, yes, I know there's nothing you can do about the satellites but still, I've put in enough complaints."

There was a sympathetic agreement from the other end of the line.

"Yes, I know you've tried all you can. What did he say he wanted?" Mindy reached for a bottle a white wine that was sitting on the coffee table, already uncorked and unfinished. She tipped it over into a nearby glass, refilling it for the third time that day. "A secure meeting? Yes, of course. You mean...

an agreement? From Hathaway's side? We've finally reached... a deal?"

Mindy brightened as she took a sip of her wine, considering what this meant. Hathaway's attorneys had folded and accepted the latest offer from Mindy's team. She was surprised at his choice, but probably shouldn't have been, considering poor Hathaway would now be tied up in an entirely *new* legal problem given his arrest. But still— part of Mindy wondered if she would *miss* fighting with her ex-husband. Something in the process had almost been therapeutic, as if she was finally releasing decades of rage she'd had to keep under wraps. Mindy wondered if Hathaway was settling because he appreciated what she'd done for him while he was in police custody. Mindy had done everything she could to ensure her ex-husband's release, even going so far as to sign a character statement. She wondered if Hathaway knew, and if her actions had somehow touched him, leading him to settle. Maybe Hathaway had changed.

"You set up the conference hall for us? Oh, thank you Alfred. You're always so kind. Yes, of course I'll be there. No, no— you don't have to confirm. I'll call him myself."

There was a muttering from the other line.

"Oh, if you really don't mind, I'll leave the confirmation to you," Mindy said. "Thank you again. You've been so supportive through this whole drama. You really are the most wonderful man."

Mindy said her goodbyes and a few more thank yous and platitudes, then hung up the phone, taking another determined sip of her wine. She turned the volume back up on her soap opera, thinking about the ways in which the events of the proceeding week mirrored the drama that was playing out on screen. She missed Tony, but there was something poetic in the fact that his final gift to her might be a new way of looking at the world. One in which petty dramas were put aside. Since Tony's unexpected murder, Mindy understood there were more important things in life than fighting. Maybe her argument with Hathaway had been a last resistance to letting go of what they had, however bad it had been. Mindy was ready to settle.

She wished Tony could be here to see her finalize her divorce. She thought about his arms wrapped around her, and the way he smiled every time he'd seen her— that crooked grin that was his and his alone. She reached for the penguin necklace under her shirt, as she so often did, and— because she was alone, and the wine was strong, and she was on her third glass— let the tears fall.

Tomorrow would be a new day.

CHAPTER THIRTY-SEVEN

HATHAWAY

HATHAWAY WAS WAITING for his bail hearing, lying alone on the hard, metal-framed bed in his holding cell. He stared up at the ceiling, trying to ignore the fact that it was the same color grey as the walls, and the floor, and the toilet in the corner. Hathaway had never appreciated how much color was present in his life until he'd found himself spending the night in a grey prison cell. He assumed it was daytime now because the lights were on, but the lack of a window made him feel he couldn't trust his sense of time. The guards could be lying to him. Maybe they turned the light on in the middle of the night to play with their captives. Hathaway would have no way of telling the difference.

Hathaway rolled over onto his side, switching his gaze to the cement wall across his cell. More grey. He thought about his tropical fish tank and appreciated it more now than he ever had. He remembered the colors on their beautiful fins. He tried to recall the exact pattern of spots and stripes on each fish, but the image alluded him. When he returned home, he'd have to name every single fish. He promised himself as much.

Hathaway had only been away from home for one night,

but he hoped Alfred would feed the fish. Tomorrow, Hathaway would use his one phone call to reach out to his parents, and would ask them to request the favor from Alfred. Alfred was the only person in the building Hathaway trusted.

Just then, there was a rattling sound outside Hathaway's cell. A guard with keys in hand was unlocking the bolt. Behind him— between the slats in the iron cells— Hathaway could just make out a familiar shape.

It was Alfred, wearing his typical suit and tie.

Hathaway blinked, sure he was imagining the shape of *Rowling Heights'* most loyal attendant. The entire scene was clearly a hallucination. But when Hathaway forced his eyes open and closed— Alfred was still standing there.

The guard slid the door open. "Your bail's been posted."

"But I have even had the hearing yet—" Hathaway started to say, his logical, legal mind taking over.

"Not sure we want to argue that point, do we?" Alfred said, a helpful glint in his voice.

Hathaway stood, unable to believe his good fortune. He pulled Alfred into a hug, surprising the man. Having been raised by a wealthy family, Hathaway had always kept his distance from the service staff. But today—when he needed someone most— Hathaway noted it wasn't his parents or his ex-wife or even his attorneys who had bothered to show up.

It was Alfred.

Hathaway released Alfred from the embrace and the two men separated, but Hathaway kept his hands clutching Alfred's upper arms. "Thank you," he said, really meaning it. "I don't know how you did it, but—"

"There were a few calls involved," Alfred smiled.

"To who?"

"Your parents. The Detectives. The Police Chief," Alfred added. "We posted the bail and convinced the judge to issue an amount without a hearing. Detective Annie Hudson was the force behind it all. She says you're not guilty and she's going to prove it. She's quite convincing when she wants to be."

"Remind me to thank her, too," Hathaway said, stepping out of the prison cell and into the hallway, glad to be closer to freedom. They followed the guard down the main escape route, pleased to see a pair of plexiglass sliding doors that marked the prison's exit.

The doors opened to a processing room, and with a couple of papers signed, Hathaway was no longer captive. He followed Alfred out the main doors into the fresh air, the sunlight outside the building burning his eyes. They stood in the parking lot for a moment, taking it all in.

"I can be honest with you, I suppose," Alfred said, tucking his hat underneath his arm. "This freedom came with a cost."

"What's that?" Hathaway bristled.

"Annie's going to reveal Tony's true killer. But she wants the entire list of suspects there. She says it won't have the same impact otherwise. I'll need you present at the meeting."

Hathaway considered this detail. At first, horror at the idea turned his veins cold. He imagined himself standing in a room with everyone who believed him to be guilty, trying to prove otherwise.

As if he could read Hathaway's mind, Alfred interjected. "Nobody thinks you did it. Not me. Not Cataline. Even Mindy came to your defense."

"She did?" Hathaway asked, surprised. "She has every reason to want me locked away, what with the divorce proceedings—"

"She told them you weren't a killer," Alfred shrugged. "She even signed a character statement stating as much."

"Those were her exact words?"

"I believe her exact words were, 'He's not a killer. He's just an idiot.'"

Hathaway grinned. "Close enough," he said.

"You'll come to the meeting then?"

Hathaway imagined the meeting yet again, but this time pictured himself vindicated, a hero in the building. He imagined the real killer being brought to justice, fingers pointed at some shadowed person that wasn't *him*. There was something juicy and delicious about the feeling. Suddenly, instead of mimicking the gray inside of the prison cell, Hathaway felt his life was unfolding in full color.

"I wouldn't miss it."

CHAPTER THIRTY-EIGHT

MONTANA

MONTANA WAS LIFTING weights in *Rowling Heights'* gym when the call came. He was halfway through a bicep curl, sweat dripping down his forehead, when he felt heard a ringing sound coming from his gym bag. He dropped the weight at once and unzipped the bag, removing the phone and answering the call.

"Yeah?"

What sounded like a polite acknowledgment came from the other line, followed by a question.

"They wanna meet with me? And they didn't give you a name?"

Montana's breath quickened. This was the moment he'd been waiting for. Finally, the people he'd hitched his wagon to long ago were going to help him. Montana had made some bad decisions. But maybe *this* one wasn't coming back around to bite him in the ass. Maybe there really was still loyalty in this world.

"No, that's alright Alfred. Not the first time someone's stopped by to talk to me and not given a name. Not your fault whatsoever."

Alfred's voice on the other end of the line came out in reassuring sweeps.

"Yes, I did tell you to send any unnamed callers my way. If they wanna meet, I'll meet 'em." There was a long pause. "Sure, set it up. Tomorrow in the conference room. I'll be there. Oh, and Alfred?" Montana waited for a response from the other end. "Might be better if those security cameras in the hall didn't work. Official DHS business. Better not to get the building involved."

Montana offered a few more "thank-yous," then promptly hung up, eager to get back to his workout. He returned to the weight-lifting, engaging in a bicep curl on his underperforming side. His breath quickened, and it wasn't only because of the workout. Montana knew this unnamed benefactor could be someone sent to help him out of his most recent mess. All he needed to do was to accept the offer.

Montana's muscles burned, but he kept curling. He knew he'd need all his strength for whatever came next.

CHAPTER THIRTY-NINE

CATALINE

CATALINE WAS MAKING dinner when the call came. She swirled a wooden spoon over a metal pot, watching as instant cheese melted over noodles. Behind her, Mario was playing a video game with a stranger halfway across the world. He shouted orders to his teammate through a headset that covered his ears, and Cataline could occasionally make out words like "blast them!" and "coming around the side!" The world of gaming was far outside Cataline's wheelhouse, but she allowed Mario to pursue what he loved. She'd noticed that— since Tony's murder— Mario had missed going upstairs to play video games with his friend. She was glad to see him engaging in the habit again, even if it *was* with a stranger halfway around the world.

Cataline stirred the macaroni in the bowl, considering her conversation with the detectives earlier that morning. She knew what was coming would be devastating. She wondered how much time she had.

Then, her cell phone vibrated. It was sitting on the countertop, the ringer turned off because Cataline tried to avoid taking calls during dinner. She looked at the caller I.D. and saw Alfred's name. She answered.

"Yes?"

Alfred spoke, his words a blur. Cataline had been expecting this, but it was still surreal, like a moment from a dream.

"Tomorrow. Yes, I'll be there. She knows who did it?" This was no surprise to Cataline either. "Did she tell you?" There was a murmur across the line. "No, no of course not. She wants to reveal it all at once. I see. Do the residents know why we're holding the meeting?" There was a long pause. "Yes," Cataline said, her heart thumping in her chest. "I think it's better not to tell them either. Reduces the flight risk. Ferdinand will be there too? I'm glad," she said, meaning it. She reached for the crucifix around her neck, holding it tightly. "That's the right thing. So many right things to be done."

Cataline wished Alfred a good evening, then hung up. She considered her options. She could run, but she'd spent too many years running. Cataline thought about what she knew of the world—how only light could drive out darkness. There was a crackling sound on the stove. The noodles were burning. Brown smoke billowed into the air. Cataline pulled the metal pot off the stove, looking at the charred remains of their dinner, the crunchy, useless leftovers a warped remainder of something that could have been great.

At once, Cataline knew what she needed to do.

"Mario?" she called out over her shoulder.

Mario stared at her from the couch. He turned off the video game without being asked. He could tell when his Mom was going to ask him to do something simple, like chores, or when she wanted to talk about something serious. He could sense from the edge of fear in her voice that this was something serious.

Cataline strode into the living room and sat next to him on the couch, putting her head in her hands.

"What is it?" Mario asked, suddenly afraid.

Cataline looked up at him. She stroked his cheek with one

hand, marveling at the way his eyes looked so much like the man she'd tried to forget. The one she'd loved instantly, so many years ago.

"I want to tell you who you your father is."

Mario stared at her in shocked disbelief, and Cataline started the story from the beginning, determined not to leave a single thing out.

CHAPTER FORTY

THE LITTLE-USED CONFERENCE room at *Rowling Heights* had never seen such a festive day. Police officers in uniform lined the back wall. Six chairs were arranged in a semi-circle to provide seating for the suspects. In the interest of maintaining the standard of luxury the building promised — even in difficult times— a spread of cold meats and cheeses was positioned on a nearby table. In front of it all, Annie and Ethan stood next to Police Chief Sanchez, their arms crossed.

"I see Alfred made sure appetizers would be available," Ethan nodded at the table.

"Not everyone's guilty, and those of us who aren't murderers appreciate the snack," Annie answered, holding a plate with the last remains of a croissant still lingering on its edge. Annie grabbed the final bit, then said, mouth full, "Five minutes and counting."

Police Chief Sanchez surveyed the scene. "We have officers in the hallway undercover as cleaning staff. A couple more in the lobby, pretending to read newspapers." She turned to Annie. "You're confident none of the suspects have been tipped off?"

"Alfred assured me he would obscure the meeting's true purpose," Annie nodded. "I trust him to abide by this with all the suspects, minus Hathaway, and one other important exception."

"And we deal with the exception— how?" Chief Sanchez asked.

"The exception will deal with herself, I expect," Annie answered cheerfully. She checked the clock on her phone. "Ah, right on time! Any minute now, we should see—"

There was a swooshing sound as the door opened and Mindy appeared on the other side, dressed in a white pantsuit, a crisp blazer dangling off her shoulders. A designer bag hung from her elbow, and she looked quite surprised to see the Police Officers against the back wall. "Oh, I'm so sorry," Mindy took a step back. "I must have the wrong room. Alfred said—"

"You're in the right place," Annie motioned to a seat in the semi-circle. "Alfred must have made a mistake. Poor man. But you're just in time. We'll be revealing how and why Tony Vasquez was killed. Given your connection, I doubt you'd want to miss such a thing."

There was a long pause as Mindy put the pieces together. She let the moment wash over her, drowning in it, then recovered as quickly as she'd sunk. "I wouldn't miss it. Never," she said, reaching for the necklace that dangled over her shirt. She glanced gain at the armed officers on the back wall. Then, she smoothed her pants and strode across the room to the table to fix herself a plate.

Moments after Mindy's arrival, Alejandro made his way into the room, disappointed to find there was no investor present. "I don't think *you'd* be interested in a Tequila-related business opportunity?" he asked Chief Sanchez, who declined immediately. When Alejandro realized he'd been set up, he first attempted to exit, but was blocked by the armed officers at the door. He followed Mindy to the food table, eventually taking his seat in the semi-circle. "If you all wanted a big reveal, you could have just been honest," he muttered under his breath. "No need to get a man's hopes up for a business opportunity."

Montana arrived soon after, taken aback by the police presence in the room. He attempted to make a swift exit but was politely escorted back into the conference area. He offered no words of protest, but instead made his way to the food table, taking a plate and placing a stack of cured meats on top. In silence, he took his seat next to Alejandro, his alert eyes scanning the room.

"How'd they get you here?" Alejandro asked, mouth full.

"Thought I'd be meeting someone that could help me out with a situation," Montana said, his voice resigned. "Seems like that ain't happenin' now." There was a sadness to his tone that imparted a deeper heaviness, as if his last chance at a great hope had just been dashed. He settled into his chair, legs open, arms folded, plate balanced on one knee. Waiting.

There was a loud bang as the door swung open once again, and every pair of eyes in the room widened at the person on the other side. It was Hathaway, a loose tie hanging around his neck, a crumpled blazer dangling from his shoulders. The group stared, each of them feeling they were looking at a dead man walking.

"My wonderful neighbors," he said, gliding into the room, arms open wide. "You didn't think I'd miss an opportunity to clear my good name?"

"Good name?" Mindy huffed. "More like an average name that was spared by yours truly."

Hathaway locked eyes with her, then marched toward her, a purposefulness in his swagger that Mindy hadn't seen embodied in her husband in decades— or, come to think of it, maybe he'd *never* exhibited such confidence. An officer on the back-wall put a hand on his weapon, holstered at his waist. Hathaway closed the distance between himself, and Mindy.

The air seemed to leave the room for a moment. Then, Hathaway did the most shocking thing he could have done under the circumstances—

He fell to one knee, took Mindy's hand in both of his, and kissed the back of her palm.

"Thank you," he said.

Mindy stuttered, unsure what to make of this new development. "It was only a character statement," she shrugged, afraid to let her guard down in case this was all a terrible trick. "You would've done the same for me."

"Not just for the statement," Hathaway said, his expression earnest. "For everything."

Mindy felt a warm, prickling energy in her chest. The two ex- overs rested there for a beat, and then the moment passed. Hathaway stood, stretching his arms overhead like he'd just awoken from a long nap, then made his way to the food table. He grabbed a set of tongs, stacking a paper plate so full of food it looked as if it might collapse.

"You wouldn't believe how terrible the food is in the big house," Hathaway sighed, taking a seat beside his neighbors.

"You were only in there one *night*," Montana growled.

"The longest night of my life," Hathaway shuddered. He took an enormous bite of the pastry on his plate. "Nothing bothers me anymore," he said, mouth full. "Not even your shitty attitude," he glanced at Montana, ".... or my divorce, or my family's expectations of me. Freedom is the greatest gift. I've got a new lease on life. Maybe I'll move to Thailand. Or India. See the Taj Mahal. Live abroad for a while."

"I've always wanted to visit India," Mindy said, surprised at herself. "Or do the *Eat, Pray, Love,* tour— see all the countries in the book."

"Perfect," Hathaway waved a hand in agreement, even though he had absolutely no idea what she was talking about. "We'll do whatever that book says. I've never read it but I will. I don't care. As long as I'm not surrounded by grey walls, I'm the luckiest bastard alive."

Near the doorway, there was a coughing sound as a throat was cleared, and everyone turned to find Alfred. He wasn't alone— beside him stood Tony's father, Ferdinand, looking somber.

"Ferdinand," Annie said, step forward to shake the aggrieved father's hand. "Thank you for coming."

"Thank *you*," he answered, "For doing what the police could not." He offered a pointed look at Police Chief Sanchez, who ushered him toward the back wall where he stood by the officers, looking out of place in the army of blue.

Annie nodded at Alfred. "You did an excellent job getting everyone here," she said. "I'm hoping we can find a way to thank you."

"No thanks necessary," he said. "Anything for the building." He took his seat at the end of the line of chairs.

Annie stood in front of the suspects:

Mindy was positioned in the first chair at the edge of the circle, her legs crossed, eyes wide in an effort to hold back tears. Alejandro sat beside her, in second position, looking riveting in one of his leather jackets. Montana was seated in third position, his elbows on his knees, his frame leaning forward with his legs spread wide. In the fourth chair sat Hathaway, still grinning from ear to ear, as if entirely unbothered by what had happened to him. In the fifth chair was Alfred, looking as poised and as regal as Annie had come to expect. Beside him, the sixth and final chair—was empty.

"I see we're still waiting on Cataline," Annie smiled at the empty chair. "We will begin without her." She cleared her throat. "You are all here because your keycard was utilized to access the penthouse floor on the night Tony Vasquez was killed," Annie began, eager to reveal her findings. "Six people in this building— besides Tony himself— visited the penthouse floor the day he died."

"One of whom is missing," Mindy pointed out helpfully.

"Cataline," Alfred whispered, his expression laced with surprise, followed by horror. He looked up at Annie. "I told her the truth— I thought—"

"As I expected you would," Annie nodded. "We've accounted for it, Alfred. Not to worry. Now, onto the business of the murder." Annie began to pace, as she always did when she was about to share a conclusion. Over her shoulder, Ethan moved to close the door, two Police Officers assisting him in the effort. The three men remained positioned by the exit, arms crossed, choking off the access point in case anyone tried to make a run for it.

"Some months before the murder, *Rowling Heights* began receiving an onslaught of strange packages. The boxes were unmarked and not designated to be delivered to any one unit. As such, Alfred stored them in the mail room. Until, of course, the mailroom was broken into, and the packages were removed. This happened multiple times until the installation of an— admittedly faulty— security camera system, which did, in all its useless, manage to capture a video of a hooded figure moving the boxes to the roof for sorting and storage." She glanced at Alfred. "Is that correct?"

"Exactly right," he confirmed.

"The cat burglar in question was storing the packages on the roof, using it as a de facto processing facility for the deliveries in question. In response, Alfred decided to block the rooftop access from all residents. Also correct?"

"Yes," Alfred nodded.

"What Alfred didn't know," Annie continued. "Was that the package thief was not the only character utilizing the roof for a specific purpose. There was someone *else* who was visiting the roof to engage in illegal activity. An activity that could only be performed from a certain height. But I'm getting ahead of myself..." She paused, standing still in place for a brief, fleeting moment. "First, let's resolve the issue of the package thief. Alejandro," she turned to Alejandro, who shrunk down in his seat. "Would you care to explain?"

"I'd prefer it if you did," Alejandro said, examining his nails as if he'd broken one.

"It might be better, coming from you," Annie urged.

"It's another business opportunity," Alejandro snapped. "Nothing but a side hustle." He turned to the neighbors, arms open in explanation. "I have the clothes shipped here from Italy. The labels have been cut off. Then, we sew on better ones and sell them. Still the finest quality. Just a different form of production."

"You buy and sell *knock-offs*," Mindy scolded, her mouth dropping open in horror. "Shameful!"

"Not everyone can afford the real thing," Alejandro said. "Who cares if it's a fake label? The product is just as good. People hardly know the difference." He paused, remembering when the idea first occurred to him. "I was pitching the liquor business in so many clubs, and I noticed the people there were all wearing designer jackets. Designer bags. I asked around and started to realize many of them were fakes. I figured I already had the contacts. Only problem is..."

"Selling knock-offs is illegal," Annie said. "Comes with quite a hefty fine if you're caught."

"Which is why I didn't put my address on the packages," Alejandro shrugged. "I figured there'd be no proof that could tie me to the crime if someone figured it out. And I sorted the inventory up on the roof to be extra careful. As soon as a box was unpacked I destroyed it, because to prosecute they'd need tangible evidence like a box where I live to tie it all to me. *Sin evidencia, sin crimen.*"

"Beyond a reasonable doubt," Hathaway confirmed.

"Yes," Alejandro nodded. "I was trying to create distance between me and the knock-offs."

"And you gave Tony the red leather jacket he was wearing the night he was killed?" Annie asked.

"He figured out what I was doing. I gave it to him to keep him quiet so he wouldn't tell Ferdinand," Alejandro cast a guilty look across the room at Ferdinand, who was listening against the back wall, taking in every word. "Told him friends don't snitch. We really were that—" Alejandro said again, directly to Ferdinand. "*Friends.* Tony and me. And I have a lotta fake friends, but Tony? I never would've hurt him."

"So Alejandro's package business caused the roof to be locked," Annie said, resuming her pacing. "Per Alfred's instructions, no one could access the rooftop. This posed an interesting problem for *the other person* who was using the roof for nefarious reasons. That's right," she smiled at their reactions. "There were *two* people using the roof for nefarious purposes. Alejandro, without even knowing it, made life much more difficult for someone else."

"I did?" Alejandro asked.

"You did," Annie said. "In fact, if the roof had never been locked off from access, Tony would not have been murdered."

Gasps filled the room. Alfred shook his head, a deep pain crossing his face. He looked over his shoulder at Ferdinand.

"I'm so sorry," he said. "I thought I was helping the building by locking it off."

"You didn't know," Ferdinand assured him. "It's alright. You couldn't have known."

"But before we get to that," Annie continued. "I'd like to circle back to someone who was thought to be our most promising suspect— Hathaway. It must feel nice, to be a free man?"

Hathaway nodded. "Never better."

"Would you like to tell everyone what you were doing on the eleventh floor the night Tony was murdered?"

"I was stealing a necklace," Hathaway said. "A penguin necklace Tony wore."

"And why did you want that necklace?"

"Because Tony and my soon-to-be-ex-wife, Mindy, were having an affair."

Shocked expression bounced across the space, and Mindy looked at the ceiling, trying not to make eye contact with anyone at all. "It doesn't count as an affair if you're separated —" she started to say before Annie interrupted her.

"—a court wouldn't see it that way. Isn't that right, Hathaway? You believed a judge would see Mindy's connection with Tony as an affair, per the terms of the prenuptial agreement between you two. Which would mean—"

"By default I'd keep everything. All our money," Hathaway said. "That's right."

"And Mindy," Annie turned to her. "We can presume we know why *you* were on the eleventh floor earlier that day?"

"I was there to see Tony," Mindy confessed. "We had lunch in the afternoon, at his place. We ate takeout. Spent a few hours together. Then, I went home."

Annie nodded. "After which, Hathaway committed his infraction." She turned to Hathaway. "The evening before the murder, you broke into Tony's apartment to take the necklace?"

"That's correct."

"And what did you do with it afterward?"

"Well, that's the funny thing," Hathaway said, scratching his chin. "I kept it in a strange cut-out in my apartment. One that was there when we moved in. A secret compartment. Nobody could have known. But then, when I was arrested—"

"They found it in your jacket pocket. Did *you* put in there?"

Hathaway shook his head. "No. But somebody must have. I mean, as far as I knew the necklace was tucked away in the private compartment in my kitchen, and then I was being arrested and it was in my pocket. How dumb would I have to be to put it in my own *pocket* and carry it around with me?"

"That is dumb, even for *you*," Mindy offered helpfully.

"What interested me about the day you were arrested was that everything seemed to fall together so neatly," Annie said, once again pacing circles over the floor. "As if right on cue, a motivation for Hathaway committing the murder was offered when Chief Sanchez's team noticed a display case in the lobby. Right there, was a picture of Mindy wearing the necklace. It all made such sense. Hathaway must have killed Tony because he was angry about the affair. But one thing struck me as odd." She stopped, turning to Alfred. "You had a teapot display planned for the month that I'd watched you set up just days earlier. Isn't that right?"

"Yes," Alfred agreed. "I was quite sad to change it. But it was suggested that a resident feature would be better for morale."

"And who made that suggestion?"

There was a long pause as Alfred seemed to fight internally. Then, he acquiesced, whispering, "Cataline."

"Who, it appears, couldn't be here today."

All eyes fell on the empty chair. On the back wall, Ferdinand took a step forward. "Cataline couldn't," he said, suddenly outraged. "She *wouldn't* hurt my son. Tell me she didn't—"

Annie held up a hand. "I'd rather she tell you herself," she glanced at her left wrist, taking in the time. "Chief Sanchez?" Annie asked. "Make the call."

CHAPTER FORTY-ONE

CATALINE

CATALINE STOOD on the train platform, Mario's hand in hers. The three o'clock train heading North would take them away from San Diego's peaceful harbor setting, moving them up California's coast straight to San Francisco. Once there, Cataline had plans to start over. A distant relative had already agreed to house them, although she wasn't sure how long the offer would last.

Cataline looked at the suitcases stacked behind them, wondering at how easy it had been to shrink their lives down into a few bags. Life was so fragile. So easy to take apart in a single moment. The idea of its transience frightened her.

There was a whistling sound as the train arrived. The doors opened, and passengers began to board. Cataline stood, frozen, her feet unwilling to move even when she commanded them forward.

"Tony was my friend," Mario said, his voice quiet beneath the background noise of the train station. "If we can help, we should."

Cataline bent down, taking his arms in her hands. "You understand what that might mean, *mijo*? What could happen—"

"There's no other choice, Mom," Mario answered. "If we don't tell them the truth, we'll just be running forever."

"If we tell them the truth, bad things may happen."

"I don't believe that," Mario said. "I think Ferdinand loves you. I think he'll understand. And even if he doesn't, I know you did everything because you love me, and the universe will protect us. *El amor todo lo puede*," he said, repeating Cataline's favorite phrase back to her as if he'd owned it all along.

"Love conquers all," she said, looking back at the train. The doors were about to close. It was now or never.

She took a deep breath, then grabbed their suitcases. Mario followed her as she marched away from the station toward the lines for taxis, ready to face what was waiting for her back at *Rowling Heights*.

CHAPTER FORTY-TWO

EVERYONE in the room waited on bated breath as Chief Sanchez hung up her phone. She announced to no one in particular:

"Attendant confirmed. Cataline bought two tickets— but she's not on the train."

"Excellent," Annie clapped her hands as if she'd been expecting this. "It seems we'll await her arrival any moment now. So then, back to the sequence of the day. We've established that Alejandro was responsible for the packages given his illegal clothing business—"

"— the quality is very high, you'd be surprised," Alejandro leaned in.

"And he was visiting Tony that day because?"

"Because to keep someone friendly you must offer favors often. I was dropping off more jackets. He wore the red one so much, I thought I could continue earning his silence," Alejandro said, no glint of shame detectible in his voice.

"We've also established that Mindy was visiting Tony in the afternoon because they were lovers," Annie said.

Mindy nodded, reaching up to touch the penguin necklace she continued to wear.

"And Hathaway was visiting the eleventh floor to procure Tony's penguin necklace to make the case his prenup with Mindy was invalidated by an affair."

"It seemed like a good idea after a few whiskeys," Hathaway clarified. "Not so much now."

"We've established that Alfred's decision to close off access to the rooftop didn't *only* affect Alejandro. There was someone *else* who was using the roof for a very specific reason. But first, let's discuss the building itself. All of you pay for a premier experience."

"That's why we chose the building," Hathaway said. "The lifestyle. The amenities. The views of the harbor."

"Ah, yes," Annie smiled. "The harbor views. Which, until about six months ago, were available in each direction from every unit. But recently, your views to one side have been obscured, have they not?"

"The skyscraper," Alejandro agreed. "They don't care they're crowding the space. This street used to be exclusive—"

"The skyscraper that's under construction," Annie said. "Which blocks a partial view of the harbor. Each of your units lost access to the view of a certain side."

"The lighthouse is over there," Mindy shrugged. She'd never cared for that portion of her view anyway, preferring the bright lights to the South. "And the DHS building. But who wants to see that anyway?"

"That *is* the question," Annie agreed. "The Department of Homeland Security Building is positioned on the side of the harbor with the blocked view— and *who* would want to see that *that?* What kind of person would find value in a view of the only water route for DHS missions? What kind of person would benefit from knowing *when* DHS boats are on the move, or in stasis?" She paused as if waiting for an answer, but no one volunteered. "Montana?" Annie asked, staring straight at him.

"As a DHS agent, maybe you could help us out with this one?"

There was a moment in which Montana considered. His life so far flashed before his eyes. He remembered the day he'd signed up to be an agent, writing his name on that form in blue ink like it was nothing. He remembered the months of training. The way he'd given it his all in the hopes he could make a difference. Somewhere along the way, the spark had faded. Now, Montana knew—there wasn't an "us" or a "them." All that mattered in life was power, and what a man was willing to do.

Moving impossibly quickly for his size, Montana jumped up, pulling a gun from a concealed carry holster under his sweater. He pointed it at his neighbors, backing up towards the exit.

Exclamations filled the room. "Trust me, you don't want to go to prison— this is ten years to life," Hathaway said, his arms in the air. "And to think we welcomed *you!*" Mindy shouted, covering her face. Alejandro dived to the ground while Alfred threw up his hands.

There was a flurry of sound as the officers on the back wall also drew their weapons, a dozen guns all pointed at Montana. Near the door to the room, Ethan and the two officers beside him drew their weapons, blocking the door with their body.

"There's nowhere to go," Annie said to Montana, tone pleasant.

"Then I'll wait," Montana shrugged. "I can take someone out with me. But I'm not going down for nothing. You don't understand that we didn't have a choice—"

A voice echoed from the front door, which Ethan had opened when he sensed a presence on the other side. "Yes, we did," Cataline stepped forward, her figure framed by an aura of light emanating from the hallway behind her.

All eyes fell to her lithe form. Her arms were shaking. She

looked smaller than normal in this context, and out of her uniform. When she was working to make the building better, Cataline appeared larger than life. But off-duty and more afraid than she'd ever been, Cataline was simply— herself.

"Put it down," she said to Montana.

He didn't answer. She walked toward him, unmoved by the fact he was still holding a loaded gun. She moved close to him, then put a hand on his cheek.

"It's over, *mi corazón*." She said. "Put it down."

There was a long pause, and then Montana holstered the gun. The officers descended upon him like locusts, their bodies covering his as they disarmed him and shoved him to the floor. Within moments, he was in handcuffs, surrounded by police who rearranged him onto his chair.

"Cataline," Annie smiled. "Would you mind taking your seat?" She motioned to the sixth chair at the end of the semi-circle, which remained unfilled. Cataline took her seat. In the back of the room, Ferdinand watched the scene unfold, unable to believe what he was witnessing.

"We were just discussing what kind of person might care about a view of the DHS building," Annie said. "Do you have any ideas?"

"A person like me," Cataline answered. "Growing up, my family was part of the cartel. It's why I came here. To get away, to start over. But they found me. And they'll use anything— *anything* to get what they want." She turned, facing Ferdinand. "They threatened Mario. Otherwise, you have to know, I would have never allowed it."

Ferdinand didn't answer. He only stared at Cataline as if he hardly knew her.

"And what did they want from you?" Annie asked.

"At first, it was simple," Cataline said. "They wanted me to report back on the DHS' movements. I let them know when the ships launched. If they were trying to smuggle drugs in from the sea, it gave them time to turn back. But then the construction started and that building across the street went up and I lost the view from my unit. I had to try the roof, because it was the only place you could still see the building, but then Alfred blocked the access—"

"And what did you do, when you lost access?"

"To be honest," Cataline admitted. "I was relieved. I couldn't ask Alfred for the key because it might have tipped him off. It gave me an excuse to push the cartel away. I told them I wouldn't work for them anymore. I said the skyscraper made it impossible to see and the roof was sealed. It gave me a way out."

"But then?"

"*I* moved into the building," Montana offered. "The cartel must have known how it would affect me to be close to her—"

"Affect you in what way?" Annie asked.

"Mario," Cataline said. "Mario is Montana's son. We met when I was coming here, crossing the border. He was working that day, and he found me in the back of a truck but let me go. We loved each other at once. But I knew I could never allow it to be, because Montana…"

"Was part of the life you were trying to escape," Annie finished the sentence for her. "How long ago did the cartel flip you?" Annie asked Montana.

"About ten years into it," Montana said. "You see so many things. So many terrible things. You start to realize it's all just about power."

"The cartel paid for you to move into the building."

"Yes," Montana said. "But it wasn't just about getting additional eyes on the DHS boats. Cataline and I put together later that they were positioning me to report back on her. They knew she had cold feet. Her father wanted her back in the game— it was all a move to get her to return. They were hoping to use me to bring her around. I didn't know, when I moved in, that she lived here. Didn't know about Mario, either. But I put it together as soon as I saw him—" Montana glanced at Cataline, then at the floor. He wasn't a man used to sharing his feelings in private, let alone in front of a room of people. "We realized we were in a situation there was no getting out of," Montana said. "Kind of like this one."

"Cataline?" Annie asked. "Why were you on the eleventh floor that day?"

"I wasn't," Cataline shrugged. "It was Mario. He used my card to go pick up a package. It was a Geneology kit. He wanted to know who his father was. I think he could feel it when he met Montana. Somewhere inside, he *knew—*"

"And Alfred deleted the security camera footage of that day because—"

"I was worried Mario would be accused of stealing the packages," Alfred said. "And then the murder on top of everything. I didn't know about all this—"

"Did the two of you try to rent Tony's unit?" Annie asked.

Cataline nodded. "The cartel doesn't take 'no' for an answer. At first, we tried to stop working with them, but they threatened everything. They sent strange men to meet Mario after school. They made sure to tell him to let me know." Cataline hesitated, remembering the late-night conversations they'd had— the way she and Montana had bartered over their options, trying to discern the course of action that would protect everyone involved. "We thought if we could find a way to keep reporting for them, it might buy us some time to figure out the best way to disappear. We pooled everything we had. The cartel didn't make the offer to Ferdinand— it was us. We knew his unit had a view of the DHS building. We thought if we could rent it, Montana could move in and keep watch twenty-four-seven. Always be on call. But Ferdinand wouldn't accept. We thought it was the most honest way to buy some time. And then—" Cataline's eyes watered and the words caught in her throat.

"And then the Cartel found out what we were up to,"

Montana finished for her. "They learned we made the offer and figured out it was Tony's unit that had the view. They told us they'd send some men to shake him up if we couldn't make progress with him."

"I didn't know," Cataline said, turning to Ferdinand, tears streaming down her cheeks. "You have to believe me. He didn't tell me until later—"

"It's true," Montana added. "I knew if I told Cataline the cartel was planning to shake down Tony, she'd pick up Mario and leave for good. I'd already lost her once. First sign of someone gettin' hurt, and I could count on her disappearing. Becoming a ghost again. Most likely without me."

"I would have, because it would have been better for Mario," Cataline said.

"So I took matters into my own hands," Montana continued. "It wasn't my intention to kill him. I just wanted to shake him up enough that he'd let go of the apartment and tell his Dad he wanted to take the deal."

"So you tied him to the balcony to scare him into agreeing," Annie said.

"I wore a ski mask over my face so he wouldn't recognize me. Just wanted him to think I was an unnamed cartel member. I tied him up and threw him over the side. I thought the rope would hold. But he took so damn long to agree. I was just about to haul him up when it happened. The rope broke. And there was nothing I could do to take it back."

"When did you find out what happened to my son?" Ferdinand said, not to Montana, but to Cataline, his voice all steel and rage. She looked at him with wide eyes.

"Not right away," she told him. "I saw Montana in the lobby earlier that day, before Tony died, and he looked shaken. He barely talked to me. It wasn't like him. I tried to reach him but he shut me out. Told me he had it handled. It wasn't until I heard Tony's scream and the car alarm went off that I began to think maybe Montana had something to do with it, but I didn't want to believe it. At least not right away. The next day, he came clean," Cataline wiped her eyes. "I should have told you as soon as I put it all together, Ferdinand. I didn't know what to do. I worried I'd lose Mario. I panicked—"

"And the two of you decided to pin the blame elsewhere," Annie nodded. She looked at Montana, "You stole the necklace from Hathaway's apartment and gave it to Cataline, who planted it on him in the hallway." Annie turned to Cataline. "And you prompted Alfred to change the images in the display case so the Police would know about the affair between Tony and Mindy, giving Hathaway a motivation."

Wordlessly, Cataline nodded. She opened her mouth to speak but was stopped by a familiar voice.

"Don't answer that," Hathaway said all at once, looking a little surprised at himself. He hadn't spoken as the mystery had unraveled itself and was now shocked to feel a call to action. "As your attorney, Cataline, I have to advise you not to answer."

"My— what?" She looked up, utterly surprised.

"Your attorney," Hathaway said, straightening his tie. "You agree, Detective, there was no answer from my client."

"I do," Annie smiled. "I heard no confirmation or denial."

"Perfect," Hathaway said. He stood, marching toward Cataline and standing by her side. "I'd like to add that the witness in question— *me*— retracts his statement as to who he saw in the hallway as he made his way to lunch."

"Interesting," Annie nodded. "And what is the witness's new testimony?"

"I didn't see anyone in the hallway," Hathaway answered. "I got it wrong before, because I was overly emotional what with being wrongly accused. I made the whole thing up. I didn't see a single person on my way to lunch, when the necklace was presumably slipped into my jacket pocket."

"Oh dear," Annie agreed. "Then I guess the mystery of who framed Hathaway will remain unsolved."

"It appears so," Hathaway said.

"I—" Cataline stammered. "Hathaway, you don't have to do this—"

"Yes, I do," he said, putting a hand on her shoulder. "You've taken my every infantile demand to heart since the divorce, without so much as a roll of the eye. You even ordered me *fish flakes*..." His heart grew heavy as thought back to the four grey walls he'd left behind. He remembered how it had felt, to have the support the building's staff provided ripped away from him. No Cataline to call with requests for assistance. No Alfred to rely on for a friendly 'hello' in the hall. "It wasn't until I lost everything, that I realized my mistakes." Hathaway couldn't help but glance at Mindy, who was looking at him like she'd never seen him before.

"Ferdinand?" Annie asked, her voice betraying a deep care for the grieving father. "What would you like to do?"

"I want justice for my son," Ferdinand said. Then, his voice softened. "But not pain for Mario."

"It was all me," Montana said, his arms still locked behind his back by a pair of silver handcuffs. He spoke directly to Ferdinand. "If you want justice, I'm the man who deserves it. Cataline didn't know what I was going to do until it was too late. She was right, when she left me the first time. And I never meant to come lookin' for her." His eyes grew hazy and far away. "I've been waiting for this moment for a while. Thought maybe the cartel would do right by me and find me a way out, but now that the moment's here... I'm relieved." He glanced at the officers surrounding the room. "I did what was right by me. You all need to do what's right by you. What're you waiting for?"

There was a subtle nod from Ferdinand, and— at his urging— Police Chief Sanchez waved a hand in the air. The officers descended on Montana, pulling him from the chair and exiting the room with their willing captive in tow.

Annie watched as the man was taken, leaving a heart-broken Cataline in his wake.

"Why?" Cataline asked Ferdinand, knowing she could never make up for the role she'd played in the murder of his son. "You should want me in jail with him. I should've told you as soon as I pieced it together. As soon as the cartel asked me to spy for them, I should have run away and not brought this trouble into the building. It was just hard to leave because, well, I love it so much. And Tony— you have to believe me, Ferdinand, if I had known what Montana was planning I would've stopped him—"

"Of course you would have," Ferdinand said, his voice barely a whisper.

"Why don't you send me off with him?"

"Do you remember what you said when I hired you?" Ferdinand asked. "I asked you why you thought you'd be a good choice for the job, and you told me it was because you would love the building as if it were your own. *El amor todo lo puede,*" he said. "Love conquers all. Mario loves you most. I cannot send you away because it would ruin the boy."

"She came back," Annie interjected helpfully. "Cataline had the opportunity to run today at the train station, but she came back. To tell you the truth." Annie motioned around the room, turning back to the remaining suspects. "Every one of you was a suspect in this crime because of who you chose to attach yourself to. Mindy was attached to Tony by love," Annie pointed at Mindy, who was clutching her necklace again. "And to Hathaway by hate," she nodded at Hathaway, who— if his expression was to be believed— agreed with her. "Hathaway attached himself to a grudge. To revenge. Alejandro was attached to the image of himself he portrays to others— that of a successful businessman—"

Alejandro crossed his arms in his seat. "I disagree, but continue."

"—Alfred was attached to his love of the building, but also to his care for Mario and Cataline," Annie went on. "Montana was tied to his son, and to the woman he never stopped loving. And Cataline—"

"— was attached to the past," Cataline answered. "It's a tie I wish I could cut. I have tried with all my heart. You have to believe me, I have tried—"

Annie smiled at Ethan, who she knew held the full power of the FBI at his disposal.

"Ethan, what's witness protection like nowadays?"

Ethan returned the grin. "Pretty nice," he said, turning to Cataline. "Especially for prime witnesses like Cataline, who's going to testify against the cartel in order to help resolve a murder case."

"I am?" Cataline shuddered, thinking of what they might do to her. She caught Ferdinand's eye across the room— saw the pain there, and the deep need to see justice served. She straightened her shoulders, standing tall. "Of course I am," she nodded.

"You'll be entitled to witness protection then. And Mario too," Ethan said. "Cataline, would you rather be a blonde, or a brunette?"

Cataline took in his words, alarmed, at first, by the idea of a change. But as the thought of a new life sunk in, she suddenly felt a weight lift from her shoulders. She imagined what it would be like to *truly* start over. She considered how it would feel to drink her coffee in the morning on the patio of a house in a small town, knowing her son was safe at school. She imagined a new name that was free from the burden of history, unfindable by those who wished to harm the only person who mattered to her. She looked again at Ferdinand.

"Only with your blessing," she said.

Ferdinand offered only a nod, but it was enough, a small movement covering years of exchanges between the two, a dance of giving and taking where neither one was ever out of debt to the other. With the motion, the song ended, and the dance was over. Ferdinand set both of them free.

Cataline turned back to Annie and Ethan. "When can Mario and I leave?" she asked.

And just like that, the case— was solved.

CHAPTER FORTY-THREE

HOURS LATER, Annie and Ethan stood beneath the exterior facade of *Rowling Heights,* a strange stillness in the air. There were no news cameras— no reporters to cover the scene. Police Chief Sanchez planned to make the announcement at the station in a few days in order to give Ferdinand time to ready himself for the inevitable onslaught of questions from the media, given his prominent position in San Diego society.

"Do you think Alfred will be happy up there?" Annie glanced eleven stories up where— against the orange streak of the setting sun— the balcony of the eleventh-floor penthouse was barely visible. Upon closing the case, Ferdinand had granted his most loyal employee, Alfred, the best unit in the building.

"Happier than Tony ended up, I hope," Ethan said. "Alfred was the only one who did what was best for the building in the end, wasn't he?"

"There's a loyalty there," Annie agreed. "One you can't buy. One that's worth more than money." She reached out, using the edges of Ethan's jacket to pull him closer. "But his love for Mario and Cataline clouded his vision."

"And?"

"Do you think your feelings for me might get in the way of the job?" Annie asked. "Your first priority has to be the FBI."

"I don't like the job that much anyway," Ethan shrugged. "Lotta late nights. Terrible health insurance. Watching you eat processed meats every lunch hour is the highlight of my day."

Ethan wrapped his jacket around Annie, keeping her warm against the harsh chill of the ocean air blowing across the bay. She leaned into him, thinking about what the case had taught her: a person's fortunes were made or broken by who they tied themselves to.

"We're a good horse and cart together," she said to him.

"Wait a second," Ethan considered. "Am I the horse, or are you the horse? Don't tell me I'm the cart..."

Just then, Police Chief Sanchez exited the building, making Annie and Ethan separate. If she noticed their close-ness, she didn't say anything— perhaps out of respect for the act of getting by. She'd spent some late nights with colleagues out in the field and understood how the craving for closeness at times overrode good judgment. She held out a manilla envelope, a proud look on her face.

"I'd told you I'd do right by you," Chief Sanchez said, passing the envelope to Annie. "One case solved, and an internal investigation of your letter in return."

Annie's heart quickened as she opened the envelope, extracting the paperwork within. This was the answer they'd been waiting for. The next step into the investigation of her brother's disappearance.

"The call about the Murder on Aspen Lane was only routed to police servers within a four state radius. Your hunch was correct — your guy is an inside man. We tracked every computer that accessed the report. The person who sent you the letter at Aspen Lane had to have accessed the open file from one of these IP addresses."

Annie and Ethan scanned the pages, hungry eyes realizing the list in front of them narrowed potential possibilities from an infinite scale to something manageable. Something feasible, with a little elbow grease.

"Thank you," Annie said. "You have no idea what this means."

Police Chief Sanchez started to walk away, then stopped herself. She turned as if something inside her wouldn't let her abandon her old friend without sharing one final thought:

"There's something that's been bothering me," Chief Sanchez said. "Not that you need my help with your brilliant mind and all, but—"

"Please," Annie said. "Tell me."

"Well, you've been solving real estate related crime for a decade," Chief Sanchez said. "This inside man— whoever he is— used the Aspen Lane case to taunt you. But there must have been other cases that were a fit for you years before that moment. So I guess my question..." Chief Sanchez chewed on the inside of her cheek, "... is *why now?*"

"I've wondered the same thing," Annie said, agreeing. "You're not wrong. In fact, I think the answer to *why now* might be very important. Thank you."

"Stay safe," Chief Sanchez answered before turning on her heel and marching toward a waiting squad car that sat at the curb, lights flashing. A door slammed as she entered the passenger side and the car pulled away, leaving Annie and Ethan alone beneath the shadow of *Rowling Heights*.

"Report's been filed with the FBI," Ethan said, hands in his pockets. "They're pleased to have two new cartel informants. Cataline is already singing like a canary, and they figure with some time they can get even more out of Montana, if he has any sense left in him."

"He'll talk," Annie said. "He'll want a shorter sentence. For Mario."

"Either way, the Bureau's pretty happy with me right now," Ethan said. "Figure I can ask to follow a lead just about anywhere. Got any ideas, boss?"

"Mmm," Annie smirked, taking his hand and leading him down the sidewalk. "I'm getting kind of tired of the city, aren't you?"

"You thinking something a little more rural?"

"I've got a friend down south," Annie said. "Might be able to help us narrow down this list." She waved the Manilla envelope in the air. Then:

"How do you feel about farm life?" she asked.

Annie didn't even need to look at Ethan to feel the horror on his face. She knew he was a city boy who preferred polluted air and a sea of grey sidewalks to vast open land that needed to be filled. Ethan like that the city offered him endless opportunities for input, allowing him to drown out the memories that kept him up at night. The city was a beast, but it was one he'd fought before. The open, empty expanses of land in most of his country made him feel small, too aware of his own voice rattling inside his head.

"A farm? I prefer to always stay within ten blocks of a Dunkin' Donuts," Ethan said, cringing.

"Don't worry. You'll be fine."

"Suspicions aren't facts," Ethan said, offering Annie's favorite phrase in response. "I'll need to see the evidence for that conclusion."

"The evidence is simple," Annie said. "You're with me."

"Right cart. Right horse," Ethan agreed.

THE END

Love Annie Hudson and want to stay on the case?

Sign up for the author's mailing list at:
www.valeriebrandy.com

Keep reading for a special preview of "Murder on the Farm,"
Book Three of the Annie Hudson Real Estate Mystery Series.

Available soon in paperback, ebook, and audiobook!

MURDER ON THE FARM

CHAPTER ONE

SOPHIA BARNAK'S corner store was a pleasant enough place-- except for the body that lay on the floor.

Private Investigator Annie Hudson stood above the limp form of a man, noting the gash on the back of his head. The wound had resulted in a pool of blood spilling out across the store's original hardwood floors, marring the otherwise immaculate space.

"Charming, isn't it?" Annie said lightly to her partner, FBI Agent Ethan Beckett. His expression informed Annie that clarity was necessary. "The store, not the man," she added, motioning away from the victim on the floor, who didn't seem to take offense at their lack of focus.

"It's cute," Ethan agreed, nodding at the original Coca-Cola posters still decorating the walls, pinned above a jukebox situated in the corner. "In an Americana kind of way."

Annie turned, taking in her surroundings. She glanced out an open window at the landscape in the distance. The store was situated on a multi-acre farm that backed up to the Dismal Swamp in Virginia's Sunray community, a Polish enclave that had been founded by immigrants many years ago. They had carved the space by hand, and what had started as untamed land was now a pleasant town of well-kept roads and bountiful farms. Sophia Barnak was one of the town's founding residents, and her store had been allowed to remain untouched for many years, standing as a reminder of Sunray's origins. Situated on the edge of a large soybean farm, the corner store prided itself on local goods. Floral, yellow wallpaper covered the space. In the back of the building, a long bar served milkshakes and sodas, a manual cash register prepared to accept payment. Wooden display shelves offered fruits, vegetables, and flowers, all harvested from surrounding farms.

"It's a cozy place," Annie added cheerfully. "Minus what happened to him," she glanced back down at their victim, finally returning her attention to the issue at hand.

"Looks like you two are legit," a husky voice rang out from the store's entryway. In the double doors stood Sheriff Chomski, the only law in town. An impressive mustache framed his features, and a softness in his eyes made Annie like him immediately. "I made some calls," he said, pocketing his radio. "FBI confirmed you're on the case, so-- if there's any thing I can do..." He didn't finish the sentence but offered a shrug instead.

"Did you know the victim?" Annie asked, eager to hear from a local.

"Sure did," Sheriff Chomski nodded. "Everybody knew him. Paul Kaminski was running the farm for the family. Sophia Barnak's relatives live out West. They're her descendants down the line. After she passed away, they needed someone to run the place, and they put Paul in charge. He's run it for decades and would be still if you know--"

"Someone didn't bash him over the head?" Ethan offered.

"Exactly," Sheriff Chomski agreed. "Wonder if this'll be a problem for the sale..."

"The property's up for sale?" Annie's ears perked up, her interest in the case growing.

"It's been up for awhile," the Sheriff said. "Finally getting interest from what I last heard. Hope this doesn't complicate things for them."

"Hope not," Annie agreed.

"Just out of curiosity," Sheriff Chomski asked. "We don't get a lotta trouble out here, but when we do, the FBI doesn't usually come calling." The Sheriff paused, evaluating the two outsiders in front of him. "Why this case?" he asked.

Annie smiled. "We made a promise to a friend," she said.

Sheriff Chomski nodded. "Then you're our kind of people," he said. "Around here, everyone's always willing to help a friend."

Annie glanced down at the victim, his body face-down on the wooden floors. "I don't know if he'd agree," she said. She paced in place, then headed for the front doors to corner store, reaching for a solid masterlock that wove between the handles, a chain dangling on one side.

"They lock the store every night?" she asked.

"That's what the family told me," Sheriff Chomski confirmed. "They let Paul manage the place and he was diligent about makin' sure it was secured."

"And there's no broken windows," Annie added, looking at the few windows that dotted the structure. "Would Paul have brought anyone here who didn't belong?"

Sheriff Chomski let out a low whistle. "No, ma'am. Paul did everything by the books. Can't see him bringing someone by to a place he didn't own. Would've been outta character."

"Then whoever did this either knew he'd be here, or had a key to building." She chewed on the inside of her lip, considering. "Call the family," she said to Sheriff Chomski. "Ask them for a list of everyone who has a key to the corner store."

And with that, her investigation began.

MORE FROM VALERIE BRANDY

The Annie Hudson Real Estate Mystery Series:

- "Murder Behind the Gates" — The Annie Hudson Real Estate Mystery Series, Book One.
- "Murder on the Farm" — The Annie Hudson Real Estate Mystery Series, Book Three.

The Predator / Prey Thriller Series:

- "Trail of Obsession" — The Predator / Prey Thriller Series, Book One.
- "Lies Run Deep" — The Predator / Prey Thriller Series, Book Two.
- "The Trap is Set" — The Predator / Prey Thriller Series, Book Three.
- "The Woman in the Wind" — The Predator / Prey Thriller Series, Book Four.

COMING SOON:

The Rebecca Orange Cozy Castle Mystery Series

- Mystery at Monrovia Castle — Book One
- A Caper in Croatia — Book Two
- Sleuthing in Scotland — Book Three

LETTER FROM THE AUTHOR

Dear Reader,

Thank you for dedicating your time to the world of Annie Hudson and the Real Estate Mystery series! I'm a screenwriter and filmmaker coming to books from Film & TV, but one thing I love about books in particular, is connecting directly with a community of readers. It's very special to be able to speak with you and hear what you want from characters in our novels.

I hope you'll reach out to me by joining my mailing list at the link below! I love to keep my readers updated on new releases, offer advanced copies, free giveaways of novellas, sneak previews, and more.

If you liked Annie Hudson, I hope you'll keep reading the rest of the series, which continues to grow! In addition, my "Predator/ Prey" thriller series is available now in all formats, starting with book one, "Trail of Obsession."

And if you want to read more from me in general, I hope you'll check out the list of my books on the previous page.

Warmly,

Valerie Brandy

Join the author's mailing list at:

www.valeriebrandy.com